Become Who You Are

SUNY series, Women Writers in Translation

Marilyn Gaddis Rose, Editor

Become Who You Are

With an additional essay, "The Old Woman"

Hedwig Dohm

Translated and with an Afterword by
Elizabeth G. Ametsbichler

State University of New York Press

Hedwig Dohm, pencil drawing by Bernd Hering, 1983; Copyright Archiv der deutschen Frauenbewegung, Kassel.

Published by
State University of New York Press, Albany

© 2006 State University of New York

For information, address State University of New York Press,
194 Washington Avenue, Suite 305, Albany, NY 12210-2384

Production by Judith Block
Marketing by Fran Keneston

Library of Congress Cataloging-in-Publication Data

Dohm, Hedwig, 1833–1919.
  Become who you are / Hedwig Dohm : translated and with an afterword by Elizabeth Ametsbichler.
      p. cm. — (SUNY series, women writers in translation)
  Includes bibliographical references and index.
  ISBN 0–7914–6603–5 (hardcover : alk. paper)
  I. Ametsbichler, Elizabeth G. II. Title. III. Series.

PT2704.036B43 2005
832'.92—dc22

2005003402

10 9 8 7 6 5 4 3 2 1

Dedicated to
Laura Ottes Graff

Contents

Preface

Often, I have been politely asked about my current research project. When I reply that I am working on a nineteenth-century German woman writer named Hedwig Dohm, the reactions I receive are unknowing nods or blank and questioning looks that precede the question: who was Hedwig Dohm? This question is typical not only of my American friends, but also of colleagues working in German literature. Few German scholars are familiar with the name Hedwig Dohm unless they have worked on nineteenth-century women's issues. In order to give people a reference point for who she was, I always add: her granddaughter (Katia Pringsheim) was married to Thomas Mann. Giving Dohm context by associating her with one of the most famous *male* authors of the twentieth century always seems rather ironic to me, because my fascination with her stems from her acerbic writings on women's rights and women's issues. Yet, this was a typical situation for pre-twentieth-century women in all fields who took a back seat while their fathers, brothers, husbands, or sons have either become famous or been recognized for their work.[1] However, many women, including Dohm, deserve to be recognized purely on their own merit, for their own lives and for their own work, as has been shown now many times in the late decades of the twentieth century by feminist scholars, who have uncovered, rediscovered, and recovered the lives and works of many accomplished women who paved the way for us.

Indeed, Dohm's first biographer, Adele Schreiber, entitled her work *Hedwig Dohm als Vorkämpferin und Vordenkerin neuer Frauenideale* [1914] [Hedwig Dohm as Champion and Pre-Thinker of New Women's Ideals]; she truly was a pioneer in the women's movement, the so-called first wave of feminism. Although she was not an activist who gave fiery speeches from the podium at feminist gatherings or meetings of the women's movement, she was an activist in her writing and thinking, a radical who wielded her pen courageously against many of the male-dominated social and political institutions of her day. What first struck me about Dohm—and has continued to hold my interest in her—is the undeniable logic with which she so wittingly deconstructs the patriarchal arguments that were so pervasive in her society. Following long traditions before them, the male, and even many female thinkers of her time argued against women's equality on all levels—domestically, educationally, politically, socially, and professionally. There were many reasons—well-known, frequently heard, and even prevalent into the late twentieth century—for excluding women from many facets of life that were open to men. But Hedwig Dohm took a hard look at these arguments and very logically and rationally picked them apart with a sharp pen and a sharp wit in her essays about women and women's issues. In addition to these essays, she focused on women's issues in her prose works and, to a lesser extent, in the four comedies that she wrote.

My continued interest in Dohm, however, not only has to do with her wit and ability to write what I perceive as riveting works of both fiction and nonfiction, but also with my understanding of her personality. She was a humble, personable, intelligent person who was often described as being very shy, but who nevertheless pursued her own way in an environment that was often exceedingly hostile. She was not only a role model for woman of all walks of life who were her contemporaries and those who lived after her, but she was a woman with whom we can identify and from whom we can learn—even on into the twenty-first century. Because I feel so strongly about her life and work, I wanted to make some of it accessible to an English-speaking audience, and I therefore chose to translate two works that seem particularly fitting as the baby boomer generation ages: her novella *Werde, die du bist* [Become Who You Are][2] and her essay "Die alte Frau" [The Old Woman].[3] Contemporary women still need champions of women's and human rights, and these two works by Dohm speak particularly expressively and movingly to these issues.

Acknowledgments

I would like to thank colleagues, friends, and family who helped me with this translation project through their encouragement and moral support. I am particularly grateful to the proofreaders of the translation; they helped the translation significantly with their thoughtful comments, suggestions, and insights. Assistant Professor of Journalism at the University of Montana, Sheri Venema, and Mohan Kartha, who worked as a professional editor in the Washington, D.C. area for many years, both helped with their careful comments on language usage. Shelley Nelson Kirilenko, Ph.D. in German Literature, assisted greatly with her bilingual eye and literary background. Most particularly, I am deeply appreciative to Linda Whittlesley, whose German upbringing and literary sensibilities were invaluable as we pondered the twists of language usage. I am also indebted to my colleague and mentor, Dr. Gerald Fetz, who always finds time to offer an extra set of reading eyes. I appreciate very much the generosity of time and energy that everyone put into this project for me.

In addition, I would like to thank the University of Montana for facilitating this project with a sabbatical award.

Become Who You Are [1894]

Hedwig Dohm

*I*n the mental hospital of Doctor Behrend, in the vicinity of Berlin, an old woman—she would have been about sixty—created quite a sensation. She had delicate, interesting facial features, thick, gray hair, and big green eyes. These eyes never stared into space. Either they were shiny, dead to the outer world, gazing inwardly at something, or they were fixed upwardly, sometimes with an expression of passionate, errant searching, sometimes fixedly absorbing some object with delight. The eyes of a seer. These wondrous eyes gave her head the character of a young woman.

Usually, she was taciturn. Occasionally, however, she started to talk; then it was as if she were carrying on a conversation with a supernatural being. Her words breathed immeasurable melancholy or dithyrambic ecstasy. She uttered profound and sublime thoughts in a form that was reminiscent of Nietzsche's *Zarathustra*.

One would have believed that this old woman had been a great poetess and that an excess of intellectual provocation caused the mental disturbance. The opposite was the case.

1

The neurologist, who was interested in this peculiar form of insanity, made inquiries about her previous life. What he found out highly astounded him and was in no way helpful in solving the puzzle of her being.

Everyone who knew the spouse of the Privy Councilor Schmidt agreed that she had been a good, well-mannered, some-what limited and philistine housewife, ignorant and totally absorbed with family life. She had two daughters who were long married. Her relationship to her children had always been exceedingly affectionate. In the last eight years [of his life], she had cared for her paralyzed husband in a self-sacrificing way. After his death, she may have felt somewhat lonely. She had been to visit her two married daughters. None of her relatives had noticed the slightest eccentricity in her, only that she appeared to them more taciturn than usual, which found an adequate expla-nation in her mourning for her spouse and in her loneliness.

But then, quite suddenly and disapproved of by her daugh-ters, she had undertaken long trips totally alone, despite her lim-ited means. Shortly after her return, her insanity broke out.

The invalid ate little nourishment; she visibly grew thinner so that her large, glimmering eyes had an uncanny effect in her pale face. It was as if the soul, which was gradually consuming, wanted to consume the body.

This old woman was peculiarly attached, with a certain tenderness, to the dress that she was wearing when she was brought to the sanitarium: a black, wool dress from the era of Marie Antoinette. Her full gray hair, a little curly on the ends, fell almost to her shoulders. In the course of the two years that she was in the sanitarium, it had become white. When they wanted to pin up her hair, she would not tolerate it. The same thing happened when they gave her a new dress in a different style to replace the worn-out one. She could not be moved to put it on. They had to have a new dress made for her in exactly the same style as the old one.

They had observed that every Sunday when the organ began to play in the small chapel, she took a wilted wreath of myrtle out of her dresser—the doctor conjectured, her bridal wreath. She decorated herself with the wreath and remained standing in the middle of the room, her hands pressed against her breast, her eyes fixed on the door with an anxious expression until the organ stopped playing. Then, softly shaking her head, she put the wreath away, covered her face with a black veil, and ate nothing the whole day.

A few times, she was visited by her daughters. They were equally as astonished as distressed by the sight of their mother. They found her totally changed in her expression as well as in her characteristics; and they were hardly capable of putting themselves into a filial relationship with this peculiar figure.

The invalid, when she saw her daughters, appeared to recollect something. Gradually, she fell into a restlessness that mounted so much that the doctor had to shorten the visit. When the daughters came a second time and the same agitation made itself known, he implored the young women to discontinue their visits for a while, but dismissed them with the hope for the recovery of their mother.

In the interests of psychological science, Doctor Behrend observed for two years now with intense attention this rare example of a disturbed mind, in which to a certain degree the disturbance had created a new individual. She felt the interest that he took in her and often fastened her eyes on him for minutes at a time, as with a searching question, a somberly painful astonishment.

One day, a young, southern German doctor, a fellow student of the neurologist, came to the sanitarium in order to observe the patient. Doctor Behrend had told him about his interesting case and gladly complied with his colleague when he expressed the wish to see the patient.

Exactly on this day—it was a Sunday—the invalid completed her sixtieth year of life. Her daughters had sent flowers; the whole room was fragrant from them.

When the two doctors entered, she was in the process of spreading the flowers on the floor. She had put the dried-up myrtle wreath in her white hair. With its sharp brown stems and withered leaves, between which only here and there a couple of dead, yellowed blossoms swayed, it resembled a crown of thorns. In her hand, she held a dried-up passionflower.

And now something totally unexpected happened. When the old woman caught sight of the strange doctor, a deep red covered her face. Pulsing life came into her shadow-like appearance, flickering light into her eyes.

"Johannes!" she said, stretching out her arms towards the stranger. Her voice sounded soft and full.

"I knew that you would come. When I wear your myrtle, I see into the distance."

She touched the wilted wreath with her hand. "On the day that you gave me the myrtle, you betrothed yourself to me. Come! Come! The white sacrificial flame is burning in the golden bowl, you know, in the cave on Capri. We dare not let him, the silver-haired one, wait. Don't you hear the metallic singing out of the depths? The sirens! The blue sea, they wear it as a jewel on the chest. They sing with blood-red lips. They sing the bride's song. And I kiss your soul."

She had spoken the last words half-singingly. She kissed the wilted flower in her hand and, slowly, without looking at him, she walked towards him.

Doctor Behrend, embarrassingly touched by the scene and worried that something unseemly could happen, grabbed the madwoman by the arm and said firmly and loudly, as he otherwise never spoke to her:

"Come to your senses, Frau Schmidt, do not forget that you are an old lady."

The invalid shuddered and looked first at him, then at the strange doctor. An uncanny change took place in her face. Precipitately, her pupils rolled in their sockets. Gradually, her features appeared to stiffen. Like a burning piece of wood that suddenly collapses into itself and becomes ashes, so did her body collapse. She would have fallen to the floor had Doctor Behrend not caught her in his arms. A deep unconsciousness befell her.

They took her to bed. When the unconsciousness turned into sleep, Doctor Behrend returned to his colleague. He assured him that the invalid had never before had such an attack. Up until now, no trace of erotic insanity had shown itself in her. He would assume that she identified his colleague with her deceased spouse, except that he had been named Eduard.

"And, my name is Johannes," the stranger countered with bleak ill-humor.

"Highly extraordinary! And that she imagined she knew you."

"She does know me. I met her three years ago on Capri. Back then, her peculiar appearance attracted my attention. She wore the same dress, or a similar one as today."

Doctor Behrend inquired as to whether he had known her fairly well.

Absolutely not. He did not remember ever having spoken with her. Even though she had sat across from him at the Hotel Pagano, she never participated in the conversation, however, it did appear to him as if she carefully paid attention to everything that he did or said. However, when he ran into her during walks, she avoided him.

Doctor Behrend asked him to share everything that he had found out about her.

"It's not very much," answered the young doctor somewhat hesitantly.

"She had a very shy nature, as if she were apologizing for her mere existence. It was odd, how different she could look, sometimes like an old woman, and then again she appeared to be barely a forty-year-old.

"Once, I met her down by the sea, at the small marina. She was having one of her young days. She bent over towards the water and mumbled to herself with smiling lips. Then she saw me and became as red as she did just now. I always get embarrassed when I see an old woman blush. I wanted to talk to her and noticed to my astonishment that she suddenly looked very old and frail. Strangely, almost angrily, she looked and turned away with a twitching movement of her arms. She did not want to be disturbed at that moment, and so I moved on.

"Another time, I noticed her on a cliff that rose straight out of the sea, but not very high. She stood tall and upright with her arms towards the back, embracing the rock. Her glances wandered over the sea with the expression that people have who are finished with this world and are on the verge of seeking another one. I stood still, in a sort of anxious suspense fearing that she could want to throw herself down. I took her for a poetess who wanted to remain incognito. An inspiration occurred to me to pay her some sort of homage. Gently, I climbed up the cliff after her and threw a bouquet of myrtle that I had freshly picked at her feet. She did not appear astonished and did not look around, only smiled and pressed the bouquet to her breast. At this moment, she had the physiognomy of a young maiden, and I fervently regretted that she was not one.

"Coincidence is sometimes cruel. When I later entered the anteroom of the dining hall where the guests were accustomed to meeting, my neighbor at the dining table, a man who was considered witty, approached me and asked if, earlier, I had noticed our vis-à-vis on the cliffs, the pure Sappho from the *Fliegende Blätter*.[1] In a fit of that base cowardliness, which against better judgment sometimes makes us the echo of the unkindness of others, I answered: yes, I did see "Grandmother Psyche."[2] Barely had this hateful mockery crossed my lips when an uncanny feeling crept over me that she was standing behind us. And, she was standing behind us. At this moment, with her opened lips and her large, staring, and horrified eyes, she reminded me of a Medusa. As if absent-minded, she took a step towards me and with a mechanical movement, grabbed the passionflower that I held in my hand and went outside. I was determined to somehow make up to her the outrage I had committed. The opportunity was not granted to me. I never saw her again. The next morning she had departed. And that I now find her again here is embarrassing for me, very embarrassing."

"No one is accusing you," Doctor Behrend soothed him, and, with a slight shrug of the shoulders, he added: "anachronism of the heart. Nothing out of the ordinary for aged women with a far too sensitive nervous system."

The stranger left the sanitarium after he had asked the neurologist to keep him informed about the further fate of the old woman.

When Doctor Behrend visited the invalid again, she was awake. She had asked that the window be opened widely. She signaled to the nurse to leave her alone with the doctor. She breathed slowly and deeply, as if, greedy for life, she were drinking the last drops from the cup of time with intense consciousness. Her nostrils trembled faintly. Her face was wholly spiritualized, every wrinkle had disappeared from it, as normally tends to happen only after death.

Even before she spoke, the doctor knew that her mind was healthy again. She held out her transparent hand to him.

"I thank you for all of your care and interest and for leaving me in peace. Here in your sanitarium, I was less insane than during my whole, previous life. I had great thoughts, saw wonderful things. Dreams and visions are indeed also life. As for Siegfried, the language of the birds was made known to me."

She pointed to a book that lay on her bureau. He brought it to her.

"After the death of my husband, I began to write a journal. I entreat you to burn it. You are a psychologist. If you would like to find out, how and why my mind became disturbed then read it before you destroy it. No one else should read it."

He took the book out of her hand.

"I don't want to be buried," she said after a pause. "Burned, in flames blazing upwardly—in flames! That I want."

And again after a pause: "Many women die on the cross, but whether only to be dead, like the poor thief, or whether for others, like our Savior?"

Her eyes looked far away, large and radiant and remained fixed on the firmament, as if she were expecting an answer from above. Then she slowly lowered herself and assumed the expression of a prophetical, most inward-looking rapture. "Yes, for the others—the other women."

She quietly moved her lips. The doctor thought that she was praying and silently left.

Scientific curiosity and personal interest in the dying woman impelled him to read the journal immediately. Here are its contents:

∞

I must write—yes—I must! Otherwise—otherwise what? I don't know. Am I suffering from heart disease? Or does it come from the brain? My insides are gnawing, the sensation of bleeding to death, of ceasing to exist, and then again the whirling restlessness. It is illness. What kind of illness?

Write I must, I certainly can't talk to anyone. And if I could, I wouldn't do it, no, never, not at any price. They would laugh, laugh about the old woman who should be happy that she has her dear life.

An old man—that is a person who isn't going to live much longer, whose days are numbered, but he lives! An old woman, however, who is poor and a widow, she is as good as dead. What does she still live for! Is this what's eating at me—that I'm still here, without knowing what for?

Yes, I must write so that I don't go crazy. Had I lived three hundred years earlier, I would think that I were possessed. By what? By the devil? But indeed, there is nothing evil in me.

Is it death? Is the wild shuttering of nature shaking me before the end? No, I am not afraid of the end. It is nothing grinning or frightening that is wearing away at me. It is something powerful, wondrously urgent, something that wants to come to light. Labor pains? What wants to be born? I don't know.

But, quiet, quiet! Indeed, I write in order to become calm.

Actually, why don't I want to become crazy? Are there not hallucinations, captivating and beautiful? If I only imagined, I were——. Away! Away! I want to be rid of it, this confusion, the black shadows, and also the luminous visions.

Coldly and matter-of-factly, I want to examine how it happened that I became like this. I want to write a sort of necrology of myself. For I am at the end. Nothing more can come. I simply want to tell the life of Agnes Schmidt who is fifty-four-years-old and has been a widow for two years with an income—life insurance and pension included—of 2,500 deutsche marks.

Something worth telling in my life? Is there anything? And what would that be?

I sat for a long time with the quill in my hand and reflected. Nothing, nothing!

Am I really Agnes Schmidt? Quite certainly Agnes Schmidt? I certainly was until my husband died. And now, gradually, it seems to me as if Agnes Schmidt is fading more and more out of my sight, into the far distance, a shadow that is before me, and that shadow is becoming ever paler, thinner, and in its place—

Quiet! Quiet! Yes, how did this come about! Indeed, from the start, everything was always organized in fixed, good order. Such a very simple, good, totally full life, my life.

I want to begin at the beginning, with the child Agnes. A well-behaved, good child, a gentle and pretty child. I didn't cause my parents any worry. I did whatever was demanded of me. However, they preferred my brother to me, and when later, I never learned music or drawing or languages or anything else, it was because my brother received everything that could be saved up for. Now I know why they preferred my brother: because he was the son and I was only the daughter. And the son caused my parents a lot of grief, the greatest when he died, barely twenty years old. I really believe that my parents would have found it less bitter if I had died. I couldn't help it. After that I became even more well-behaved; I barely had time and opportunity to be any different. My father's salary—he was chancellery councilor—was small. Mother and I, we faithfully held everything together. Barely twelve years old, I helped with the household, in the kitchen, with the laundry, in the free time that I had from school. I did it all gladly; it didn't even occur to me that things could have been different. All girls who lived in simple circumstances like we did, did pretty much the same. I was cheerful, content, and very healthy. The private school where I was sent must have been inadequate. I neither learned to write with correct orthography, nor really anything else. And yet, I thanked this school now and then for the Sunday mood when we read the classics. Once I had to recite a Schiller poem. I did it with glowing cheeks and so solemnly that the whole class laughed. I was ashamed of myself, never did it again, and from then on monotonously recited the poems just like the others did. I've apparently always been shy and sensitive.

Similarly, it excited me when at night the moon shone on my bed. I got up, climbed onto the table that stood in front of the window and, with a throbbing heart, looked out into the silver dream world. Once, the table toppled over. There was great clamor in the house. I was punished and learned that I had done something very bad. And when the moon again wanted to tempt me, I pulled the bedcovers up over my head. This is how they taught me to recognize what good and evil is.

I often dreamed that I could fly, far, far away, and as high as the sky is. Then I felt annoyed when I woke up. It had been so wonderful, the flying. My mother was certainly a good woman. I don't know much more about her. But I do remember that she rigorously paid attention to order and decorum. What others did, that was the right thing for her. It would have bothered her had my dress been a few centimeters longer or shorter than those of the other school children. We dressed according to the calendar, not according to the thermometer. Mother essentially lived only for father. He was presumably somewhat stunted. He barely took any notice of me. He didn't know what he should talk to me about. I think that he considered only sons to be rightful children. Since parents are always disappointed when daughters instead of sons are born to them, girls had to be subordinate.

From time to time, I was allowed to read on Sunday afternoons. When I was grown up, I very much liked to read the novels of Marlitt. Marlitt's novels and, on holidays, apple cake with whipped cream, these were the extra joys of the daughter of the chancellery councilor.

When I was still very young, a young civil servant who worked in my father's office courted me. My parents thought that he would be competent and upright and suitable for the demands that a simple girl without means could make.

I liked him; an engagement I liked even more. What tempted me irresistibly, however, was the idea of the white satin dress with the train, of the myrtle wreath, and of the veil.

The marriage was still so far in the future. What it would be and what kind of demands it made on women—I didn't inquire after that. And no one taught me about it.

In composed cheerfulness, the four years of my engagement passed by. During this time, I was even much busier than before. I sewed my whole trousseau, as is proper. I learned to cook and do tailoring in order to be prepared for any situation, as my mother said. And evening after evening, my groom, Eduard Schmidt, came, and I cut and buttered bread for him, and he appeared to me to be so clever, because he knew so much about which I had no idea.

I really liked Eduard. I think that every person has to really like someone; for me, it was Eduard.

One day, however, it was time for the wedding. After a short honeymoon, we moved into a small apartment on the ground floor on Philipp Street. The rooms were located on the north side. The sun never shone in.

During the first part of our marriage, I was less cheerful and satisfied than during the engagement. I also didn't like Eduard as much. I suppose I am naturally cool and shy, and my inner being balked at much of what belonged to marriage. After I bore him two children, Eduard understood that his salary would not be enough for an even larger family. And from then on we lived peacefully and were together in a cloudless marriage that lasted thirty-three years.

Now, when I think back on him, I think that he was an honorable man, a total bureaucrat. He always held the opinions that befit him as bureaucrat, not out of love of service, but out of an honest sense of duty. He had as much affinity with my mother as possible. That he was convinced of his superiority over me, was somewhat willful and strict in his demands on me, did not disturb the peace of our marriage. I never opposed him, rather arranged everything quite as he wished it. In the interest of his family, he had bought a lot of life insurance. Thus, I had to work diligently in order to make ends meet. I did what I could; it also really wasn't too much. All young women who married bureaucrats without means did the same, and I did it gladly. Indeed, I was accustomed to it from my youth.

Towards evening, I was always ready to go walking with Eduard. But he usually walked so fast that it was strenuous for me. He liked to play cards before going to bed. I didn't like to play cards, was happy, however, that I could perform this small service for him. And then I was so tired and slept so well. I was healthy, my husband was happy and satisfied, my daughters Grete and Magdalene blossomed. Hearty and lively children whom I loved with my whole heart, but who saw to it that I had to work vigorously.

And one day was like the next. As if on wheels, my life glided forward, quickly, quickly. Only when I had to sit at the sewing machine for a couple hours straight did I get nervous. Then I sometimes had a strange sensation: a rippling shiver in my nerves. The thread broke, the needle fell out of my hand, and I sat up and took notice, as if something had to happen—what, I could not have said. A vague astonishment about the woman who sat there at the sewing machine and so busily stitched, a sudden feeling of estrangement in the dear, familiar surroundings. But it always passed quickly.

I really lacked nothing except that I got to read so seldom. I liked to read so much. But I consoled myself with the thought that when my girls were grown and married, then I would have time, so much time to read, whole afternoons and evenings.

And they did grow up, and I was able to read less than ever; because now they were socially active, and we had to reciprocate the invitations. Preparing their toilet, concern about meals totally absorbed my time. This was also the time when my heart often would become heavy, for the sake of my girls. One time I was afraid that Magdalene might become engaged to a foreigner whose character offered no guarantee for a good marriage. Another time, the idea tormented me that the young factory owner, who had courted Grete so long already and to whom her heart belonged, was perhaps only playing a reckless game with her. This anxiety and uneasiness lasted for three years, a time in which I was totally engrossed in the sufferings and joys of my daughters. In the end, everything turned out for the best. Grete married the young factory owner and Magdalene [married] a judge of the District Court. Distressing for me was that neither of the two stayed in Berlin.

Privately, I was somewhat amazed that they had given their affections to these particular men, but was happy indeed to know that they were well provided for.

More cheerful than ever, I looked towards the future. Grete and Magdalene wanted to visit us often in Berlin, and I wanted to go to them every year with Eduard.

And, we would travel. Eduard promised me that. Until now, we had only occasionally had a summer vacation for four weeks in the vicinity of Berlin, in Misdroy or in the Harz, where we regularly took the servant girl so that we could economize. This had resulted in some stress in the small bathing resort. I had always had twice as much work. And afternoons, when walks were taken, I was already tired and preferred to stay at home. And if I sometimes accompanied my family, my thoughts still remained behind with the servant girl, with the evening meal; also I had to exert myself in order to keep up with the others.

But now, everything was supposed to change. We now had enough money. We wanted to travel far, far away, to Switzerland, to Tyrol. Maybe even as far as Italy.

It wasn't meant to be. A few weeks after the marriage of our daughters, Eduard got sick. He didn't get well again. An infection of the spinal cord developed that bound him to his sickbed for eight years. For eight years I cared for him. With the loving stubbornness of a sick person, he would take nothing, not even the smallest assistance, from anyone except me. He ate only what I myself prepared for him and was even dissatisfied when I had to leave his sickroom. Poor, poor Eduard! Never had every hour of my life been so filled up as during this long illness.

There could be no talk of a trip to my daughters. Now and then, they did come to Berlin for a day. But everything was so sad in the house; I didn't even have a moment's time for them, so that I didn't dare to try to persuade them to stay longer, or visit more often. The factory of Grete's husband was in the vicinity of Magdeburg, and Magdalene's husband was a judge in a small town near Hanover.

In the course of the eight years, they presented me with four grandchildren. I didn't get to meet them.

I only fleetingly saw my sons-in-law when they accompanied their wives to pay a short visit to the poor invalid. I was so awkward and didn't know how to extricate myself to do something for their amusement.

Eduard died. I fervently mourned him. In the beginning, it was incomprehensible to me that he was no longer there, that I shouldn't take care of him any more. During the day, I ran restlessly through the rooms, always listening in case he should call me. Often, when I woke up in the night, I rushed to his bed. Everything around me was still, empty.

My daughters had wanted to take me with them immediately after the funeral. I had asked them to let some time pass until I had become more composed. They understood and let me be. I had to promise to come as soon as possible.

I was still busy for a few weeks with putting the estate in order; then I was done with everything. I was tired from the hard, daily work of the past years. I was allowed to take a rest. Why did rest not come? It didn't come. And now it started, quite gradually—the strangeness, the gnawing, the ruminating, the frightfulness.

I sat for hours and did nothing and just dozed. Then I ran from the apartment onto the street and from the street back into the apartment. I had such an aversion to visiting my daughters. And they couldn't come to me. Grete was expecting her third child; Magdalene couldn't be done without for one day in the household. She also knew that I was well, I lacked nothing. Right—what then?

I had written my daughters that I would come in the spring, but in the spring, I wrote that I wouldn't travel until fall. They answered that I would be heartily welcome at anytime.

Everything had been so good in my life. No serious trouble had afflicted me. Even Eduard's illness had been a gentle, gradual, almost painless extinguishing. At the last, he had been so happy when he received the title of *Geheimrat*. It had done me well to care for him.

Now, I learned to read, read as much as I wanted. And I read novels like the ones I used to love, in the style of Marlitt. I don't like them any more, I often read mechanically without knowing what. I am so indifferent as to what is in them, just so indifferent.

I did delicate embroidery for the clothes of my grandchildren. Grete and Magdalene thanked me very nicely for it, but I read between the lines that this kind of embroidery is no longer fashionable. And I should save my poor, old eyes, they write. My poor, old eyes, however, are still quite healthy. I gave up embroidering.

Now what? I water the plants, which have enough water; I wipe dust from the furniture on which no more dust lies. I often stand in the middle of the room and look around me for something to do. How ugly my room is! So many crocheted doilies! I pick up the crocheted doilies and put them down again. I've gone to the churchyard daily and have gathered the wilted flowers on Eduard's grave. When I noticed that these walks to the churchyard were just habitual, I gave them up.

∞

Yesterday, I by chance glanced in the mirror. I was shocked. My God, I was indeed an old woman. So many furrows and wrinkles. How long have I been this way then? How quickly this happens. Until now I had never thought about my outward appearance. How inadequate and tasteless my dress was! The black, wool dress with the long waist, the narrow sleeves, and the black, silk apron on top of it, the small, outdated, white collar with the large porcelain brooch upon which Grete's image had been painted, but not at all like her. And the black netting over my flat, pulled-back, gray hair. Ugly and old! That was I.

I often stand for a long, long time at the window and watch people go by. Odd, that no one knows I am standing up here and watching. And no one knows about the other; no one knows anything about anyone.

Did I know a lot about Eduard? What did I even know? That he liked to eat scrambled eggs and ham and that I always had to put his handkerchiefs, numerically ordered, in the dresser, otherwise he would get angry.

And he,—what did he know about me? Indeed, there wasn't anything to know about me. We were both upright people who did their duty.

And this frightening restlessness now, as if I had a bad conscience? Whom did I ever hurt? Or is it after all because Eduard died? At first, yes, then the shuddering astonishment about it, his death, overcame me. But now, his facial features have almost disappeared for me. Violently, I want to press my thoughts towards him; they find nothing to which they can cling. I want to think about Grete, about Magdalene. But it is only the children, the young girls whose pictures I have in mind. I don't know their lives as women. I look at the photographs of my grandchildren whom I've never seen; I am incapable of grasping the idea that they are the children of my daughters.

I search for memories from my childhood, from my married life—nothing. I read Eduard's letters—nothing. The letters from my daughters—nothing! Nothing!

But still, there has to be something, anything at all.

I give up occupying myself. I don't sew any more. I eat what the maid happens to put in front of me. I don't water the plants anymore. They dry up. Incessantly. Indeed, I'm also drying up. When friends from the past visit me and they talk about household things, then it becomes difficult for me to listen to them; I don't comprehend that in the past my thoughts hung on such things as turning old material and utilizing left-over pieces of meat. If they come again, the old friends, I will just not be at home. I want to be alone.

There is something in me like a vague memory of something distantly remote, from a long, long time ago, perhaps only in dreams that I used to dream and have since forgotten.

Mignon,[3] who had never seen Italy and yearned to go there with all the fibers of her heart. The feeling of *Heimat* was in her blood. Am I also such an old Mignon who—yes, I am searching for where I am at home. Strange idea: an old Mignon with a large porcelain brooch and—

I have found where I am at home, have to be at home—at my children's. That's where I belong. I won't write anymore. I want to meet my grandchildren. Magdalene was always so sweet and thoughtful. Perhaps I can talk to her about my shattered nerves. She will certainly have some advice. Tomorrow already, I will leave. I'm looking forward to it, I'm very much looking forward to it.

∞

Eight weeks later.

I will indeed write again. It's only gotten worse. I was at Grete's for four weeks, and now I've already been at Magdalene's for a whole month. Now I know the kind of madness for which I have a tendency: paranoia. My daughters, my sons-in-law, my grandchildren, all of them dear, excellent, cheerful, and happy people, and yet—yet—I wish that I were away once more, at home. Everything in their homes is so solid, so matter-of-factly light as day.

Right away it made me nervous that my dear children still call me "*Mämmchen*."[4] "Mother," a nice word, "*Mämmchen*" is as if they didn't take their mother seriously, only as a comical, old woman, as if it didn't oblige them to anything. And Eugen and Heinrich, my sons-in-law, call me "*Mamachen*." Big, grown-up men, strange men call me mama. It must be the custom. Grete and Magdalene, were they really still wholly my daughters? They follow in their husbands' footsteps in all ways. They speak with their words, they hear with their ears, they have adopted their opinions and habits.

It is good, very good that it's like this. But, they have indeed become quite new people, and I am self-conscious in their presence. My slender Lenchen is now heavy, Grete has developed into an honest to goodness woman of the world, and she is so clever. I'm amazed at her cleverness. She intimidates me somewhat, and Heinrich, her husband, he intimidates me too. And yet, he has so much goodwill towards me, he's always concerned about my health. Whenever he took a walk or paid a visit with Grete, then he thought that it would not be something for *Mamachen; Mamachen* would certainly much rather stay at home with the grandchildren. He also didn't permit me to expose myself to the evening air. And since they usually ate outside, I preferred then to eat the evening meal an hour earlier with the children. He simply doesn't want to believe that I am still quite strong and healthy.

I noticed that it was often embarrassing for Grete when I spent so much time in the backrooms. I put her at ease, I liked being with the children best. It wasn't quite so. I just prefer being with the children. Despite all of the counter assurances, I still can't get rid of the feeling that I hamper my sons-in-law a little in their domestic intimacy, if for no other reason than because I am their mother-in-law and also old and a bureaucrat's widow.

In the beginning, I often went into Grete's living room in the evening and read the newspaper there. The paper crumpled somewhat. I saw that it made Heinrich nervous.

If only I could at least do something for them!

For my Lenchen, who lives in simple circumstances, it would certainly be agreeable if I sometimes looked after the children or the canning of fruit, which I used to understand so well. Ach, I have become so listless about everything and also just so tired. Recently, when I wanted to bake a cake for one of the children's birthdays, it turned out badly, and the children descended on me with teasing. They danced around me like small savages and sang the popular song: "We Don't Need Any Mama-in-Law." And everyone laughed, the grown-ups too, and it was also really so very comical and yet—yet—Here I am always only called the mother-in-law, and actually, I am here as mother.

Is it also not comical when the little ones complain about me to their mother: the *Großmämmchen* took cookies, or the *Großmämmchen* looked at herself in your mirror, mama. And little Walter does not want me to have strawberries at the dinner table because then there won't be any left over for his nanny.

How they all always amuse themselves by that. Not I. I've become dulled, dulled. I don't even have a sense for the naïve roguish tricks of the little ones. I had imagined a grandmother otherwise, the children probably did too. They didn't particularly like me. That's quite natural. I'm not funny, don't bring them anything, and don't know any fairy tales. Just because I am their grandmother and old—that's certainly no reason to like me. They often play war. Occasionally, I have to play the enemy whom they stab to death. And they stab and hit me so valiantly with their little wooden spears that they seriously hurt me, but I laugh and act as if I find it charming, otherwise they would tolerate me even less, the cute mad fellows. Recently, when I forbade little Walter something, he said: "I won't obey you, you're only just a widow!" Wise child. A widow, that means: your husband is dead. You've been buried with him. The Indian widow-burning does indeed have a deep meaning—still today, and not only in India.

I am no personage. I am no one, that's also why no one can like me, even my children—barely—barely.

Now and again, I wanted to give Grete advice concerning domestic organization. However, she asserted that it had been so in my time, now everything had become more efficient. Or she didn't answer at all, only nodded pleasantly to me and probably thought: why spend any time contradicting the old *Mämmchen*. And Magdalene, she always had the same objection: "But Eugen says—" and Eugen really does say—. Psst! Mother-in-law!

Once I had spoken with Grete about a naturopathic treatment for children's illnesses. Then Heinrich stood up and said: "Please, mamma, anything but medicine." And the next day, we talked about education for girls. Then he stood up and said: "Anything but education, then preferably medicine." I no longer know what I should talk about and am becoming silent and monosyllabic; I only say the most simple things, about the weather, about the thriving appearance of the children, and I say it only mechanically so that they don't view me as sullen and dissatisfied.

At times I catch myself talking out loud to myself. Do old people perhaps do this so often because others don't want to hear them?

Another time, when Grete was having a social gathering, I had put on very fine, new gloves in order to be a credit to her. "Do me a favor, *Mamachen*," Heinrich said, "and take off the gloves, then people will immediately see that you belong to the family." For a moment it occurred to me: did he have the ulterior motive that with my meager appearance I would be compromising as an invited guest? One is not responsible for a mother or mother-in-law. One has to accept her as God has made her. I immediately regretted this thought.

He loudly praised my good heart to his guests, how I so faithfully cared for my spouse for eight years. This was distressingly embarrassing for me and really hurt me. And again I thought: is he by chance praising you as a way of apologizing for your otherwise wretchedness. I do say it—paranoia.

When I come home from a walk and an especially distinguished guest is visiting my children, then I go up the back steps, quietly, so that no one hears me. It's uncomfortable for them to have to introduce the old *Mämmchen* to the guest, and after that, they don't know what to do with her. It bothers me that I am so helpless, so undignified with my gray hair; the few polite phrases that visitors now and again direct at me irritate me. They indeed don't need to talk to me. They ought not to.

My Grete was so affectionate at our parting and Heinrich so benevolently friendly, if somewhat absentminded. The children blew a fanfare—the sweetest whim of all—or—humor, old *Mämmchen*! Humor!

I cause Magdalene so much inconvenience. She did without her carpet because of me. Recently, she complained of cold feet. "But why then do you have your carpet?" Eugen asked. She winked at him. And then I noticed that at noon, she didn't drink her glass of wine as usual. She limited herself in order to give it to me. Recently, it escaped her, unintentionally.

Magdalene is as I was. I see myself in her as in a mirror. She, too, often doesn't take anything from a dish so that her husband will have quite a lot of it. Except, she proceeds with everything more practically. She knows how to arrange it so that her husband figures out when she sacrifices for him. I was always afraid he [Eduard] could notice it. And she does everything more quickly, lively, and consciously than I did it. And her husband—she loves him quite differently than I loved Eduard, quite differently.

He is funny, Eugen, totally inclined to joking. Both of my sons-in-law are inexhaustible with their mother-in-law anecdotes. Eugen in his funny way is always so surprised by my appetite. What *Mamachen* can eat! Enviable! By the way, Heinrich is also surprised by it. He considers my fervent appetite a downright characteristic of mothers-in-law.

It really does seem that I eat an unusually large amount. It was embarrassing to me. For a while I took pains to eat little; this was considered advantageous indeed. Recently, however, I must have eaten way too little. Perhaps there was also another reason, but I felt weak enough to die and had fainting fits. I asked Magdalene for a glass of red wine and, if it wasn't too much trouble, a little meat. How Eugen was amused by that. He couldn't stop laughing. An illness that could be cured with red wine and beefsteak, he wished he also had such an illness. And he told this to everyone who visited and caused a lot of merriment with it.

They live in simple circumstances, have no worries, and yet Eugen recently said: "*Mamachen*" has it good; she can fully economize. He doesn't find it right that I live so alone in Berlin, since they have such a pretty extra room. It's also incomprehensible how a single old lady could spend almost three thousand deutsche marks on herself alone. Why, for example, the large apartment with three rooms, and so forth.

Magdalene admonished him. After all, I had the money in order to make my old days pleasant and comfortable.

Naturally, he indeed also wanted that *Mamachen* had the best, and he certainly was not making any claim on Lene's share of the life insurance. But if he were to invest fifteen hundred deutsche marks annually for me—he had the opportunity to invest the money well—then, with the saved-up money, I could afford an extra pleasure for myself, travel or do something similar. "And then you can buy me a rocking horse," little Walter interjected, "bigger than any other." I should think about it, Eugen said, my little reserved room would always be ready.

It really was only a small room, a very small one. I was afraid that he could demand a positive promise from me, and I didn't want to give it.

When that evening I expressed my joy about the fragrance of the linden blossoms, he said: "Try to contain yourself, *Mamachen*." And he said it so comically that everyone laughed again.

Recently, we went for a ride, the horses took fright and reared up high. I acted afraid. "May God's will prevail," said Eugen laughingly in order to joke away my fright. "If anything should happen to you, *Mamachen*, your daughters are well taken care of, you have two charming sons-in-law" and so forth.

Such jokes always make me sad.

I was the saddest a couple of days ago after I was taken ill by a sudden, violent sickness. And Magdalene had the doctor come. Eugen listened, so curiously intently, to the remarks of the doctor. Why then? To live, when someone wishes that you were dead— horrible! Horrible! But he doesn't really wish it. I am only—I have only—

Recently, I heard through the open door, how a man said to my son-in-law: "What, Mama Schmidt is still living? I have never heard anything said about her." And, what should they have said about me!

Humor, *Mämmchen*! Humor!

I'm mad at myself that Eugen's jokes bother me. In the past, I was indeed gentle and unpretentious. Does one lose these characteristics with age?

My sons-in-law are excellent, and I am sincerely thankful to them that they make my daughters so happy. But, I must leave, yes, I must! I'm no longer restless, but every day, I become more apathetic. Mentally, something is falling asleep in me, like one's hands and feet getting numb. All the blood is leaking from my brain. I have to exercise it, exercise! Into the outdoors. Into the outdoors!

Maybe children are indeed only an episode in a woman's life, and they quit being daughters when they have become mothers. It is almost an anachronism that they still have a mother. Also, they live in another time, in another circle. That's why a mother is out of place at her children's.

No, I more likely could have spoken to any stranger about my nervous, overwrought state than to my children. They would have immediately thought that I was on the way to losing my sanity. Would they have been totally wrong?

Tomorrow, I'm departing. I'm looking forward—What was it I had wanted to write? Ach, God!

∞

At home again. Now it will get better, much better. I'm no longer as if numbed. I am awake, almost adventurous. I go out a lot, I go to galleries, to the theater. I read, yes, mainly I read. I have found books mentioned in the newspaper, Russian, French, Scandinavian, that are supposed to signify an intellectual and moral shift and portray life as it really is. How it really is? Would it be worth the trouble of portrayal? I read in these books, for days. At times they captivated me to pathological excitement, to shivering emotion. Then again, I understood nothing more. If I wanted to hold onto a train of thought, it dissolved once more. I also didn't take the time to read page by page attentively, I only leafed through the books. Indeed, I don't have any time. I want to grasp the spirit of the whole, in flight. It's as if I am hounded by something that is always after me—what? Death, mental confusion, or what else?

A national migration [*Völkerwanderung*] of ideas, moods, thoughts is crashing in on me. How? These authors are repudiating that which until now was considered irrefutable—customs, opinions, beliefs, morals! They also claim that woman is not a subordinate creature predestined for a lower function in life! What's this for me! Now! What! I throw the books down and then take them up again. Gradually, I understand them better, and slowly, slowly they open up a new, strange world for me, like stars plunging out of evening fog. And then, I again have the odd sense that once before I had had all these new thoughts that are found in these books, as if they had latently rested in me somewhere.

Now, if only the belief in the transmigration of souls were no empty delusion!

I really like to read the books where women, driven by fiery idealism, accomplish heroic, sacrificing acts. If I could have become such a woman, if—. And I was a maid my whole life!

✿

I have discovered something new about myself—vanity. I have never known what vanity is. I had become engaged so young. Eduard had no sense for appearances. He didn't even notice if I looked good or bad. The only measure for my dress had been its cheapness and durability. And, if the material could be turned. Now, charming and graceful clothes catch my eye on the street. Perhaps my sense for beauty has also been awakened by the many pictures that I see. Do I really have to be so ugly? I had a dress tailored for myself out of fine, black wool, which is long and falls in pleats over my feet, with a shawl over the shoulders, exactly as I had seen it in a picture of Marie Antoinette. I let my gray hair, which is heavy and fairly short, fall freely on my shoulders. I also thought about pinning on a flower, an inconspicuous one. I tried it out with a small violet. I immediately threw it away. It looked so childish, as if I wanted to appear younger. Anything but that.

When now at dusk—it has to be dusk—I walk through the room, pass by the mirror, then I look as if I were someone, anyone other than the good Frau Schmidt and no longer old, and my heart throbs, and I look around me as if I wanted—if I only knew what? At times I have to laugh inwardly, as if I had fooled Agnes Schmidt, the stranger that I wanted to be. If I go out during the day, then I put on my old clothes again and imagine that I am wearing a disguise, and when some old acquaintance greets me, I am almost amazed that she has recognized me.

Evenings, I often go out without my hat. Only a scarf on my head. I now always have the tendency to free myself from a variety of things. I myself don't really know from what. Also from the crocheted doilies, they are all gone now. I have bought as many flowers as I could, intensely fragrant ones. Then when I close my eyes and it is so fragrant, I dream about all of the fairy tales that I wasn't allowed to read in my youth.

In the past, I had never visited portrait galleries. Now, at first, I went dazed, confused through the halls. Only gradually did the pictures start to have an effect on me, at least individual ones, in front of which I remain standing again and again, most often in front of Böcklin.[5] I love the clear fairy-tale splendor, the supernatural quality of his colors, the golden trees, the purple garments, the radiating ether, the holy flowers. Yes, gods, priests, and dream figures belong in this nature. Even his animals have a mystical, dreamy character.

Why didn't Böcklin paint Lohengrin in the skiff that the magical swans are pulling? Why not Siegfried's funeral procession over the heath; music is his color, now shawm sounds, now a requiem or a chorus. I'm discovering that what captivates and moves me is only that which lies beyond the real. Suspense of the dim distant, of the wondrous. Or do I perhaps clutch at such excitement like the proletarian at alcohol because he can't have substantive nourishment? Do I want intoxication?

∞

I go for long walks. Previously, I would only go out to run errands. But now, I really go walking, slowly through the zoo. For days now, the weather has been dreary and full of rain. Air and sky gray, always gray. The leaves that are still green, faded and black-spotted. The ground covered with brownish and dirty yellow foliage; in between, broken-off, decayed branches. Something musty in the air. The damp, heavy earth appears to absorb the leaves into itself. Yes, it nourishes itself from them. This is now my fate too, to die out like this, in mustiness and gloominess, sucked in—

In a remote area of the zoo, there is a small, chaotic, fenced-in garden, I think with a little gardener's hut in it. I went in. In a corner stood a decayed sculpture made of sandstone, totally enveloped with late wild roses, red roses, purple-red. I pulled the roses apart in order to see what kind of statue it was. It had no head. The column was speckled, totally red, as if blood from the headless trunk had dripped down on it and the roses were so flaming red from that.

It was as if I knew to whom the head belonged that was missing from the column, and I had only forgotten it. I searched for the head in the bushes. And every time I come back to this spot, I automatically search for the head. And automatically, I feel for my own head. But it is still there. Only no longer quite so firmly attached.

In the zoo it is now so bleak. I would like a view into the distance, open, faraway from the city and people. I would like fields and meadows.

Not far from my apartment one comes to the avenue that leads to Wilmersdorf. I went there. Yes, open fields! On one side, greenish-gray earth, ugly patches of sand with growths of short grasses, here and there a bunch of weeds or a pine shrub, in the distance a row of thin trees.

On the other side, I don't know if there were fields or construction sites or storage places for various things. Stale air. No fresh breeze. Junk strewn over the whole field, broken watering cans and old boots. Piles of dung, a few linen rags, bricks. At another place, tangled growth from potatoes and a piece of lattice fence; next to that, purplish refuse from rotting cabbage heads. A garden shed made of boards, loosely slapped together and draped with some blackish, dirty material, and behind that a sunflower. A crippled tree, under which a decaying cart stood. A work cart with emaciated horses being loaded with the last potatoes and cabbage heads. Brown undergrowth, gray, blackish undergrowth, misty fog, [and] in the distance the back houses of tenement blocks.

Unnerved, ill-humored, I sauntered down the desolate, boring street.

An odd wagon slowly came towards me, a small apartment on wheels with windows on every side. White curtains on the windows and brown heads of children that cheerfully looked out. They were gypsies who traveled from place to place. A barely grown-up, young thing came hopping up to me and begged—no, she didn't beg, she tried to persuade me with impish charm to give her something. I asked where they were traveling. She laughed and said: "Further." Didn't they have a fixed residence? She laughed again. They were born in the wagon there, they married in it, had children, and they would die in it, always on the road.

And this girl, who wore a sort of ball dress with flounce, picked up out of the trash, danced in front of me, with a blossoming zest for life, beauty and charm in every movement. Nothing gloomy and dull in these gypsies. I wonder, is it their boundless freedom to which they owe this nimble grace, their joyful security without human fear? I wonder if this is the right thing? Always onward, from place to place, sleeping in a different spot every night, today in airy heights, tomorrow in the depths of the forest, on wide, sunny plains, on the shore of the rivers, in the womb of the mountains!

It is a horrifying notion, the idea of always having to stay in the same place while there are millions of more beautiful places. Never to see them! We are miserably organized. So totally without wings.

Involuntarily, I left, as quickly as I could, forward—forward!

I came close to Grunewald, where on the edge of a skimpy pine forest there stands a row of pubs. People from the lower classes tend to stop there.

In front of the woods was a field which was broken up by wilted potato weeds. The black, damp earth showed through the thin grass. Here and there, small piles of clippings and trash. New construction still with scaffolding. In the distance, the city's masses of buildings. It was Sunday. I hadn't thought about that. Butcher and baker carriages with numerous families stopped in front of the pubs. Young people bustled about on the meadow, played hoops and tag, the young girls with flowing hair in light dresses of bright colors, a lot of sky blue and rose red. The parents sat on a pile of rock and ate the buttered bread that they took out of their baskets. The mothers had feathers or colorful flowers in their hats, next to them their crocheting or knitting. Behind them umbrellas. All around them greasy wrappings. In the restaurants: snapshot photographers, shooting stands, hurdy-gurdies, and carousels. In a restaurant yard, a bear performed. Drearily, heavily, nobly did the fall sky hang over the garish cheerfulness.

The incessant firing of guns, the smell of beer, the hurdy-gurdies that played ever more passionately, the carousel horses that galloped around ever more wildly with the merry girl riders, the shrieks over the bears—was this not dissolute, senseless! And so close to the dust of the highway and without sun!

What do they need sun for? Yes, youth is sun. And age—its mild, clear quiet, is that also not sun? Sun in the winter. It doesn't warm. I want real sun, southern sun, summer sun. I want—be quiet! Quiet! Old Mignon! In Berlin, in an ugly, sunless street you lived, and there you will remain and die.

Shivering, I contemptuously turned away from the shrieking merriment. Behind me, a young fellow called: "Hey, young woman, how's it going?" Boisterous laughter.

I notice that I sometimes arouse the ridicule of people, and don't know why. It irritates me. I suffer from the secret fear that they could notice the contradiction between my inner and my outward being. Indeed, they have decreed how a person is supposed to be at every age of life. That's why, when I see people coming, I stoop over so that I appear even older than I am. I give myself a dull appearance as if I am more or less just vegetating, as is proper in my years. The *old man* is an amiable idea, the *old woman* an unpleasant one. If one really, bitterly wants to offend someone, then one says: you are an old woman.

An old man, if he is wise, knowledgeable, good, noble-minded, is valued according to his worth. Deeply thought sayings, even if they were carved in runic character in ancient stone, remain valid according to their contents. However, if a living, old woman were to speak or think the wisest and noblest things, it would be spoken into the wind. And whoever judges her in a friendly way, says: too bad that she isn't younger.

Is it not shameful that people consider the noblest characteristics of a woman to be the spice of her young body?

So contemptuously, so reluctantly do people look at an old woman, as if her age were a fault that deserved punishment. You young ones and younger ones, but you too will grow old, and you want to grow old, and you consider it a cruel fate not to get old.

Why do you contradict yourselves so?

Does a person then live only for a certain period of life? Is childhood only overture, old age only epilogue? Certainly, not. Also childhood, also old age have the full, complete right to exist. A person, even if he were only an eighty-year-old woman, has just as much right to live as a twenty-year-old. Do you know whether he might not be worth more in his eightieth year than he was in his twentieth?

The antipathy towards old women reflects much of the barbarism of earlier times, eras in which illness was also considered to be a fault, and when people simply drowned the aged when they could no longer work.

Are there no saints at whose feet we can lay down our suffering? Holy future! You, do plead for us old women!

∞

How lonely I am. As far as my thoughts reach, there is no person who is there for me.

But yet, I want to be lonely. I feel myself brought down to earth, pulled downward as soon as I hear human voices or steps and wait impatiently until they have receded into the distance.

No, I can never go among people again. I again simply doze for days at a time. And then suddenly I start up out of my waking dreams with nervous shaking. But, I do suffer; I suffer! Is this the compensation for the goodness of an entire life?

Was I really so good and dutiful? I could indeed not have been any other way! Perhaps I was only so tame because they had tamed me from childhood on.

Once I looked out at a remote road, close to a guard house, down a long stretch, trees in all possible and impossible forms. The gatekeeper had made artistic wire netting in his spare time into which he let small trees grow. There one saw a lyre, a chair, a crown, an eagle, and numerous other objects. I wanted to laugh about them. But before I started laughing, I became pensive. A finished frame into which one forces trees to grow. How perfectly successful this piece of art was. Whether trees, whether people, this piece of art will always succeed. Training! The shepherd dog and the breeding dog, indeed they are also good and dutiful.

They had chained up my nature. Now I've been unleashed, and I wander about in the new, strange world and would perhaps cause mischief, but there is already a new chain—age.

Living for others ought to be the right, the true thing. If that were so, and everyone lived for others, then indeed others also would have had to live for me, and then it just would be the same and much simpler if everyone lived for himself from the beginning. A mother ought to be there only for the children! So I should only live and work for my daughter, and the daughter in turn should only be there for her children. What a senseless, fruitless circular course.

Did I really only have duties towards others, none towards myself? Were all of the others more worthy than I? If they had been, then—then of course—

Did Eduard have the right to say: live for me! Did my parents have it? My children? Had I fulfilled the duty towards myself and developed my intelligence, then through my clarified reason my children would have advanced in their thinking, and they, in turn, would not have become as I was. Our duties! Shouldn't they be such that they make us better, nobler and not the other way around? Are they allowed to push us downwards onto a lower niveau? Much of what they impress upon us as duty is quite certainly not our duty, for example, the duty to belong to the spouse, even when our nature rebels against it. And if this is a false duty, why not many others too that they demand of us in the name of duty.

Love your neighbor as yourself, it says in the gospel.

I am allowed, I ought then to love myself? What have I ever done for myself out of love? Nothing that I knew of.

But yet I was always satisfied? I? But I wasn't even an "I." Agnes Schmidt! A name! A hand! A foot, a body! No soul, no brain. I have lived a life in which I wasn't even present.

Is this totally true? There were indeed very beautiful moments in my life, when the children were small, such sweet creatures.

Now, however, they aren't even my children any more, they are the wives of their husbands. They have disappeared from me.

Perhaps all of my inner need comes from the fact that my father was a chancellery councilor and my mother the wife of a chancellery councilor and that I had a little too few drops of iron in my blood; the anemic blood could not move the brain's nerves.

Who and what am I, actually? I'm curious about myself.

It often seems to me as if sparks from some fire touched me, a sun that I don't see. I blow into the sparks with all my strength, so that they become flames. My breath is so short. They die away, the sparks—ashes.

∽

Today I had gloomy moments, thoughts about disastrous things, about death. The many flowers in the room, half wilted, exhaled a stale, flat odor. I had read for a long time, everything pell-mell, philosophical, scientific texts, and had tormented myself with separating the images of ideas out of the chaos.

Everything quiet around me. Only the ticking of the clock. It got dark in the room—night. A dull strip of light from the street lamp fell on the low, white oven upon which a vase stands. It looked like a funeral urn.

A short while ago, I saw a picture: a person in a casket. He had lifted up the casket lid and stared upwards with glassy terror. Horrible! Will he have the strength to lift up the lid completely and climb out of the casket, or—it's falling—falling—

I had the same feeling, as if I lay in a casket and, through the lifted-up lid, saw a little piece of sky, a small piece; and with the inexpressible yearning to encompass the wide horizon with my eyes, I pushed and pushed against the lid. And I felt, my strength slackened, my thoughts failed, and slowly, slowly—the casket lid—it fell—fell—— In terrible fright I sprang up, I put a scarf on my head and rushed outside. A cool, clear December evening.

Yes, the wide, great star-filled heavens above calmed me. Now, I almost wondered about the shudder within us regarding going home, disintegrating ourselves into immeasurable eternity. What is then in me that would be valuable enough to exist throughout eternities! Just let the lid fall, old woman!

∽

Outside in the open air, I find peace. As soon as I'm within my four walls, it starts up again, the confusion, the sensation as if my head were only loosely attached. Sometimes I hold it, I hold it with both hands. I cannot think what and how I want to. It's as if ideas, pictures, images were intruding upon me from without, hot and wild, too many! Too many! The space in my brain is too narrow. They suffocate each other. I feel their convulsions. Death convulsions? To make you insane.

Insanity—is this something different than the blocking of ideas; visions that come to us and that emanate from us, we know not where to and where from, and over which we have no power?

If this is insanity, then I was insane for more than fifty years. I always quietly held the intentions, the opinions of others. According to the natural law of gravity, the apple falls to the middle point of the Earth if it finds no resistance. Thus, it seems also a natural law that the will and power of others over us find their limit only in our resistance. I was a mechanism that strange powers set into motion. And now, I am wrestling myself out of this insanity. I'm wrestling, wrestling for my will, for myself, for my "I."

∽

Again, I've not written in the past four weeks. Something so unexpected has happened. An old relative, from whom I've heard nothing in decades, has died and left me ten thousand deutsche marks. Ten thousand deutsche marks! Such a large sum! I'll give it to Magdalene's husband. He needs it so badly, and he's so very attached to money. Certainly, he would also be thankful. Maybe then he would not begrudge me the few, poor years that I still have to live. Yes, I want to do that. This is the right thing to do.

Giving others happiness, that is the best thing. I don't have anything else with which I could give happiness.

Eight days later. No, I won't give Eugen the money. I have struggled and struggled. Now I have decided. I'll keep it. I want to use it for me, totally for me alone.

I want to travel, far away! Into the wide, wide world! The pressure on my brain will lessen. I'll conceal the money from my children. I want to see the sea! How I will love it, the sea, the great sea and then—then—Italy!

Indeed, I know only sunless days and long, long evenings by kerosene lamp. Never have I seen morning dawns and evening sunsets with open eyes, never—

Is it very wrong that I'm keeping the money? Do I want happiness? Desire? Yes—a little. But above all, I want to go for-ward—upwards! Be rid of the small housewife soul, catch a glim-mer of the large world soul [*Weltseele*]. It's an ethical wanderlust—really? There's also something mean about it, I know it. A sort of revenge because of the wrong done to me. Revenge? On whom? Indeed, I did everything voluntarily. No one forced me. Ignorance of the law does not protect against punishment in bourgeois life. So it is, it appears, also in the sphere of spiritual life. I didn't know the laws of my nature and violated them. And the punishment: lifelong prison? No, I want out! Only a few drops from the cup that quenches the thirst for life, the last drops.

Tomorrow already—T O M O R R O W.

Eight days later. I'm still here. Yes, there is something wrong about this. I can't get rid of it. My conscience—

Or do we perhaps only have pangs of conscience when we do something that stands in contradiction with that which is held by general opinion to be good[?] Otherwise, why would we so seldom have a bad conscience because of bad thoughts, rather than always only because of bad actions[?] Why does the conscience not affect one who kills a person in a duel when he knew perhaps that he shot better than his opponent[?] This was indeed murder. But because others do not see it as murder, but rather view it as totally permissible, his conscience thus remains silent.

There are, however, consciences that are more finely and acutely organized and that free themselves from the collective conscience of the larger group[.] For example, a woman who lives in a degrading marriage with a bad man and who courageously follows the man of her love, despite not being able to move her spouse to agree to a divorce. This woman surely wouldn't have a bad conscience. But yet she still would always agree with the moral elite. Or Charlotte Corday.[6] General opinion branded her deed as murder; however, a fanatical community exonerates her as a heroine.

But what if I were to do something that I thought was the right thing and whereby I wholly, totally stood alone? For example, if I made it clear to Magdalene that her husband has a base mind and puts her down, and I demanded from her that she leave him, and she were to do that and fall into inner and outward need because of it—would not, not only the general judgment, but also my own conscience be against me? And in this case, conscience would indeed be a misnomer for a yearning to return to the fleshpots of Egypt.

I'm keeping the money; I'll travel.

Quite certainly, my heart and mind are fixed not only on distant countries, but even more, much more on distant thoughts, lofty thoughts. I yearn inexpressibly for knowledge, for pure reason, for insight. I would like to think all thoughts, feel all feelings. And there is a crossbar in front of my brain. What kind of thrillingly sublime pleasure it must be to pile up thought after thought until they literally touch the stars and the riddle of the universe (*Welträtsel*).

Must one, like Faust, always sell oneself to the devil in order to know? Why can't one sell oneself to Heaven?

Recently—am I writing this?—I—drank champagne, secretly, behind closed doors. I wanted to drink power, mental power, into myself.

In vain! I remain downcast.

Think! But I have not learned to think, and one must indeed learn that. I really don't know what has been thought by me. When I think that I have gotten ahead, I'm only just there where others have stood long, long before me. I can't talk. But write? Writing comes naturally to me, as if I had done nothing else from my youth on. Ideas, images force themselves onto me in chaotic abundance. And yet—I also cannot write what I would like to write. That's because I'm not even half, hardly a quarter educated. I want different, soaring words, more finely constructed sentences. They are there in my head—locked up. I rattle, rattle— in vain, the key bolt does not give way.

And the ideas, they come wrapped in fog and mist, blurred, aphoristic shadows. They are lacking sun, brightness. Everything is only intuition, momentary understanding. Lightening and darkness.

It must be the same for a mute person as it is for me, who wants to speak, speak with the highest effect, and he cannot, cannot.

And no one helps me, no one. I am alone.

The knowledgeable have had years of learning and wandering. They have explored countries and people, they have studied whole libraries, they have hung on the lips of wise teachers. He who wants to go to the heights must climb step-by-step, and he must have guides. Wanting to fly without wings: nonsense! Megalomania!

Or no nonsense after all? Could one disregard everything that had been thought until now and move beyond generations of epoch-making genius to produce creative thoughts out of the depths of one's own soul? I tried to do it. I have reflected and reflected upon the purpose of our existence and found nothing more than the platitude that man has no other purpose, cannot have any other, than a stone, a plant, the earth: to become, to grow, to pass away.

Certainly, a plant is more than a stone, an animal is more than a plant, a person more than an animal, but not much more, not much.

And even if I could also perceive and find what the best people of all times have perceived and found, it wouldn't be enough for me, not enough.

How far can even the smartest and wisest think beyond his era? Perhaps fifty, perhaps a hundred years, if he is a seer or a genius.

Would not this consciousness have to paralyze the strength of those who want to go upwards? No. The restless upward movement is indeed an instinct; it is a sunny, a compelling natural necessity, a known one, just as the tree has to produce a new ring every year. It is not at all in our power not to refine, not to perfect ourselves.

And this instinct of refinement is what drives me away, and I must follow it, yes, I must.

∽

Eight days later.

At the sea! The North Sea! A strong, northerly wind rages around me, it revives the body and soul for me.

> I always just wander along the shore, farther, farther.
> A dune juts out, I want to know what lies behind it
>   —the sea again.
> A new bend—farther—farther! Always the sea, the
>   same, the same.

No, not the same after all. Early in the day, the waves still caressingly flattered the land, and towards evening, they seized it with gigantic claws, roaring, choking as if they wanted to tear it to pieces and bury it in its dark womb.

The raging work of these immense masses of water—what does it create? Nothing. Afterwards everything is as before. And our raging? The same. Afterwards everything is as before. And the sea still rages, and we still rage.

My head is becoming free, my chest wide in the harsh, powerful air. Is it then agreed upon that I am old? An old woman? Perhaps I am an exception of nature. So few things have been proven. That precisely this is proven, that we get old and have to die! But indeed one can become a hundred years old! And I'm only fifty-five. I still have almost a half a century ahead of me.

Get up! Afresh! Go out! Wander!

And I walked cheerfully for probably an hour. Ahead of me was a young girl in a red dress. Then my breath got shorter, my strength waned, I merely dragged myself along, and in bitter disillusionment, my gaze followed the young girl in red until in the distance—ach, in such far distance, she was lost.

No, I am no exception, I won't get to be a hundred years old, I will—I will nothing. I am a thing begun that will not be finished, never.

∞

The sea is the most beautiful in the hours that precede night. Evenings, when the tide has withdrawn, then the sun's reflections are mirrored in the gently trickling water on the shore with a sweet, silken-soft glimmer of endless tenderness, bluish or pink. This sweet halfheartedness in the color of the water, the spongy soft shading has an effect like fading Aeolian harps, or like the breath of a sigh of love on a flute.

So must old age elapse, a gentle, echoing evening prayer.

There is something touching about the flakes of foam that the surf casts onto the sand and that now, out of their element, trembling, freezing, remain behind until the sand absorbs them. I am also such sea foam, torn out of my element, and the sand absorbs me—today—tomorrow. What is then still left of me? But I live still and feel the cold.

∞

Today in the lightless twilight hour, a cold wind blew. Densely gathered clouds in the sky. The sea greenish, night-like. The shore desolate and wet. The broad colorlessness illuminated only by the white foam. I felt the cold to the marrow. And yet, I stood as if spellbound. And when later I entered my warm, friendly room, I appeared to myself as if dispersed from the cosmos; I was drawn back to the colorless beach, out into the immeasurable, the colossal. And in the presence of this grandiose unkindness, in this distant mood of the universe, I lost the feeling of my personality and floated away with the waving surges out into the vastness.

I often have the secret feeling that I no longer know if I exist and who I am. Then I utter to myself the name Agnes Schmidt a dozen times, out of fear that I could forget it. I and Agnes Schmidt? What do we have in common?

∞

I like to seek out a narrow spot on the beach enclosed by high dunes where there is nothing but the sea, the gray sea with white crowns of foam. When a strong wind blows and the flying sand darts along the shore in an uncanny hurry like something living, and the gray-green grasses on the dunes flow trembling into each other, then I feel enveloped by a great, melancholic loneliness as in a penitential robe.

Indeed, I am a repentant one. Whose guilt am I doing penance for?

Chaotically, thoughts rush over me in confusion. A chaos out of which there are flashes and rumbles. Sometimes a heavenly light emerges, sometimes through a crack, I see hell yawning.

Often, when the strips of flames in the sky are reflected in the darkening metallic sparkle of the water, and I lie half asleep by the sea, then I do not know whether I'm dreaming or whether I'm having visions.

Today, it was as if I were standing in the air on a bridge of rays. A procession of geniuses, crowned with roses, floated towards me strewing flowers amidst sweet song. I stretched out my hand for the flowers. Then suddenly out of the dark clouds, a wild chase rushes to the spot. The demons gasp their icy breath, and the breath becomes a storm. And it deafens the song and whirls the flowers and geniuses away. And me with them.

I tumble down, and I lie on the shore with a wound in my breast. The sand drinks my blood, and long, reddish grasses spring forth, sharp as swords. And the demons have become furies and threaten me—what do you want—you from me?

Avenge a dead one? A murdered one? A soul? But, indeed, I am the victim! The victim am I. Unhappiness is not guilt.

The last glimmer of the setting sun went out. The vision disappeared. I want to view spirits! Spirits! And I only see ghosts. Or am I myself—a ghost that sees ghosts! Utter lunacy this!

∞

Storm! Storm on the sea! The unleashed wildness does me good. Black clouds chase over the horizon. Suddenly, a fearful, pale sun breaks forth, but already new clouds chase after her and extinguish the tender light. The few trees on the shore bend, whimpering like a living thing that is being whipped. More! More! I love these trombone sounds of the air, the howling hissing, the shuddering jubilation. Giant sighs, as if they wanted to burst open the breast of nature. In this dithyrambic lust is both the highest affirmation and the denial of life. Madness and enthusiasm is in this storm, something that wants out of the narrow orbit of our small planet. Yes—out of it! Upwards!

In this storm at sea it has become clear to me. Now I know it. I know it for certain; I will call it out into all the winds: murder of the soul! Who committed it? No one. Everyone. My parents? My husband? No. They are innocent. That I was born a hundred years too early, that's it. When my time comes, I will be dead, already long decayed; to be born at the right time and in the right country, everything depends on this. That I was born in Berlin, that's the beginning of my misfortune. In southern Italy or in India, where palm trees rustle and the sun never sets, that should have been my homeland (*Heimat*).

What should have become of me? A painter, perhaps? Yes, thirstily, with fervor my eyes hang on the countenance of nature. I understand its gentle and wild language. Oh, but, I cannot even use a paintbrush.

Or a writer? I look, imagine, think. I would like to create, create out of the depths of my breast. There runs a spring, but I have no receptacle with which to scoop, and the living waters trickle off, trickle off, and my heart blood along with them. I can cry, bitterly, but I cannot describe the tears. What I feel, it's as wild as the sea, rushing, immeasurably deadly. I cannot say it. Lessing says that Raphael,[7] even born without hands, would have become the greatest painter. Perhaps. But he would have ended in suicide or insanity. At times, I thrust out a loud cry, a "woe," as if I belonged to the chorus of a Greek tragedy, but only when the sea loudly roars so that no one hears it, not even I myself. It is so ridiculous. For I am only an old widow. The orphan child.

∽

I am in deep, deep distress! Whom do I call? Prayer? Yes, I would like to embrace the cross, some holy symbol. Ach, I was not born in order to believe. Heaven is too low for me, faith too childlike, too selfish.

Higher, higher upward grows my boundless yearning, towards worlds where no decayed body buries the flaming soul. Always to have to! To have to live! To have to die! To have to think so rigidly! I want freedom! Bodiless, limitless freedom!

Why did I have to live as I have lived? Because I am a woman and because it stands written on ancient, bronze tablets of law how a woman ought to live? But the text is erroneous; it is erroneous!

> Why has no one erased the erroneous text?
> Because one cannot erase letters of bronze?
> Then one smashes the tablets like Moses
>   did on Sinai. One smashes them!
> I had a vision again.

I saw a long procession of swans gliding over the water. Their white plumage glowed in the rosy evening light. And the swans sang their swan song with such deathly sadness, so heart wrenchingly that the sea bed below was moved by their singing. I saw all of the tender, colorful starfish and the silver-glistening fish under the surface of the water gliding in a jumble, and in the middle of them, a head emerged, the head of a dead person, a drowned person.

Horrid. Reeds in the white, dripping hair; in the empty eye sockets, phosphorescent light.

And shuddering, I saw, the head—my head. But no, it was the same head that was missing on the statue in the weathered garden. Also my head? I'm holding it, I'm holding it with both hands, firmly.

And then suddenly I knew it. Yes, for a long, long time already, I've had suicidal thoughts.

The sea is pulling me down. The northern wind has too highly strained my nerves, strained them to the point of rupturing. I must go away, to where mild breezes blow, where there is sun, and the wind stirs the palm trees.

Italy!

Eight days later.

In Florence. I won't stay here long. No place for me. Flowers and singing and cheerfulness and gracefulness.

A country for the young. I stand out here. And yet, when I climb up to the magnificent square of San Michele and the church of San Miniato—I do this almost daily—and [I] am glowing through and through from the sun and beauty, then the thought sometimes occurs to me that I could still occupy a place in the world, perhaps educate children in a cloister. However, when I'm in my room again an hour later, then the fire is extinguished. It was indeed only a reflection of the Florence sun. I collapse weakly.

I saw a girl who scooped water out of a marble basin. She wore a red blouse and a light-colored skirt. It was with the utmost gracefulness how, standing on her tiptoes with her upper body bent forward, she caught the clear jet of water in a copper container. Her black hair hung chaotically over her forehead. Her dark eyes laughed. Blossoming life. Blossoming body. What did this girl remind me of? I approached her; involuntarily my glance fell onto the water surface, and I saw her image next to mine. Quietly, I crept away from there.

I don't know why I suddenly had to think back on my sixteenth birthday. On that day, I wore a white dress and a dahlia in my hair.

Eduard wanted to visit. I had stepped in front of the mirror, but only to fasten the flower; I didn't think about my appearance. And now, after forty years, this reflection surfaced out of my memory, a face with radiant, dark eyes, a heavy, black braid, and blossoming, rosy colors. Yes, I had resembled that girl from the basin. A bitter woefulness dampened my eyes, because I hadn't known that I was beautiful and young.

∞

I had wanted to leave Florence immediately. And now I can't tear myself away. I'm quite taken with the magnificent gardens of the Pitti Palace and the Boboli Gardens.

And this palace, it has stood for centuries like a rock in the surf of time, and for centuries the wind has rushed through its evergreen oaks.

> Rock and tree, I envy them.
> To be! To be! Anything but not-being!

That I should make such a commotion about myself! What does the individual matter!

But the species passes away just as the individual does, only it takes somewhat longer. The earth will cool off, and people will no longer walk on it. The time frame is not worth talking about when one compares it to eternity!

Thus, I am right to cry about myself, that my awakening arrives now too late, since all is in decline. The wrong that was done to me has been done to everyone. Whatever it is in me that wants to be freed wants at the same time to free others. If you hinder the growth of a tree, you also kill the fruit. You kill the shade that would have refreshed others.

Often I count the minutes in frantic fear. How few are still left me! Then Agnes Schmidt dies. But I! I too?

A vegetating natural existence without intelligence, is this not really the best happiness? A boy is in the house where I am staying, barely eighteen years old. He sits all day outside on the steps of the staircase and sings, sings like a bird in the branches, always the same, the same melody, sometimes in a sad, sometimes in a cheerful manner. I don't ever see him sad or annoyed, always just with an expression of happy cheerfulness. And the reason? A few brain cells less than other people.

Is not madness indeed much more a piece of pure nature than our trained reason? Madness lets impressions and ideas have an effect, as the sun affects the plants, as the storm affects the sea, without criticism, without resistance.

∞

I like to be in churchyards. There our thoughts resemble the thoughts we have when we are sick. Everything futile disappears. We become clear-sighted. I love listening to what the dead speak.

In the churchyard of San Miniato, however, there they remain mute under their ugly graves, graves that are reminiscent of junk rooms.

Small, raw iron bars with metal rings for flower pots enclose the tombs. In the flower pots are skimpy, dusty artificial flowers, black or white. Wreaths hang on the iron bars, or they lie on the graves, wreaths of ugly pearls or straw flowers. Small, silly things are there, little vases, lanterns, every sort of childish junk. And all this in view of the magnificent Apennine Mountain range on the distant horizon, which evening after evening glows purplish-violet in festive glory in the presence of the nobly beautiful church with the dark cypresses.

How simple and natural it would be, only a green hill upon which Florence's sun shines. Yes, upon the hill. But it wouldn't reach as far as the dead.

We always seek the heights in life. And now—down below—so far down. Does God come to us HERE BELOW? Surely we have to go to him UP ABOVE!

I don't want to be buried. Burned. In flames!

Yet, they surely will not burn me. I don't want any flowers on my grave, no stone, no tree—nothing. It is such a childish, superstitious impulse, as if the dead ones knew that one lets the flowers wilt on their mounds, that one brings them no wreath on the day of death. We think that we aren't really totally dead as long as a living person still thinks about us.

∞

The Boboli Gardens—perhaps the most beautiful gardens on Earth—are made completely out of green walls. Laurel trees, cypresses, evergreen oaks. They stand on hilly terrain. In them, one climbs up and down. Secluded from the world, one wanders between these airy walls that emanate a pleasant fragrance, the deep-blue sky above. Here and there they lead to an opening from which one looks towards the mountains and down onto the sea of houses of the city. In the womb of the mountains, villages and cities; solitary farmsteads up to the tops of the mountains. In the evening light, they glisten like sparkling precious stones on flaming veils.

Breathing here is a pleasure. The fall aroma of the trees blends with the fresh breath that comes from the mountains.

Characteristic of the gardens is also the mixture of art and nature. Sculptures, mostly out of marble, some out of sandstone, everywhere.

They stand in recesses and in open areas, they push up out of water surfaces, they beckon and entice out of green hiding places, they stand out in the atmosphere of air.

A wide, proud avenue of high towering, evergreen trees leads downwards from one of the plateaus to a water surface, from which the godly figure of Neptune looms. The trees stand there like pillars. Statues rest against them, gods and goddesses, joyful and lively, in lovely sublimity. An avenue, as if it led to Parnassus or to an Elysian field.

Near the exit of this godly street, avenues branch off from both sides such as I've never seen; wide, but low, green arcades, the treetops of the evergreen oaks closely entwined, so thick that only ducky golden sunbeams dart in. The green roof, an arch of pure architectonic form; the trunks that bear it, fantastic columns. Temple halls, loges of God.

At the one end of this temple hall, a marble goddess rests in a triumphal carriage. Her gleaming white body is enticing. I went to where she lured me and came to one of the most beautiful spots in the park, to a rather precipitous avenue.

Now I sit there dreamily, often for hours, surrounded by walls of laurels. At the foot of the avenue is a grass plot with a remainder of old ruins. Beyond the grass plot, the terrain rises gently with groups of deciduous trees in autumn finery of bewildering beauty.

The dark, harsh green of the oaks and laurel trees appears only as background to this dreamy, inexpressible tenderness of color. Sheerest gold tones that have greenish, yellowish, and reddish, even flaming red tints play and gradually gently flow into one another. A picture of color that appears woven out of light, love, fragrance, and dream; a picture of the gentlest and most enchanting ingenuity, of caressing, spherical charm. A rainbow that once spanned above appeared severe in comparison. Hushed silence. Only now and again a soft, gentle breeze as if it were coming out of mysterious heights and bringing a holy message. Even the ringing of the bells from below appears too profane for the Olympian character of the gardens.

I once heard how someone in the park said: "Nothing but trees, this is not really a garden, this is a blended, unsuccessful forest. Where then are the flowers?"

This is true. The Boboli Gardens have no flowers. And this is their peculiar feature. Only trees and stone. They need no flowers; they should have no flowers. They don't belong there. Flowers are an image of transitoriness. They wilt overnight, like people too. That's why people don't belong in these gardens either, which are somehow immortal as if created for eternity. A hundred years ago, it was exactly the same as now, and after a hundred years, it will still be so: serious, large, classic, lonely.

∞

Today, I am writing in the gardens themselves. The rosy glow of the sky quivers on the water surface of the pond, and

Neptune and all of the other godly figures bloom out of the rosy ether. Here, I comprehend that beauty, properly speaking, can be an object of adoration and that those barbarians who prayed to the sun were right.

Under cypresses we lament differently than under blossoming lindens. No sighs. No screams like at the sea. The dark cypresses point towards the sky. Pain becomes solemn sadness, it becomes prayer. A quiet losing of oneself like the sound of a bell in the air.

I would like to live in one of the small, little houses on the way to San Michele, forever. There I want to pass away to eternal peace.

I sat still for a long time.

In the face of this clarified beauty, astonishment seizes me, a melancholic astonishment about how people think that they were created as the most noble of all.

How? In the universe, a tiny planet, the Earth, is a charity case. She receives her light and her warmth from other planets. And upon this planet is a microscopic small being: the human being.

And in the infinity of the universe with its countless suns and planets, precisely this creation is the one around which everything else is centered? This the crown of creation?

Not likely.

If the Earth were to disappear from the world, and with her, all humanity, maybe the universe would be no more deeply moved by that than the Earth is by an earthquake in Sicily.

But if the sun ceases to exist, then dead stars are plunged into eternal night.

And we helpless creatures, with eyes that cry, with hearts that break, with sickness and torment, we who once were not and once will not be, we—the highest?

I can't believe it.

There must be worlds where no eyes cry, no hearts break. There must be beings without misery and need, beings that are not dust and that are eternally in sunny happiness. A happiness as we intuit in ecstatic moments with shuddering rapture.

> Just why do I ruminate about it? The stars are so
>   very far, so far.
> Yet on earth, the human being is the height
>   of creation. Really? Is he this?
> He is more than all of the daisies around me
>   that are so wonderfully lovely?

The color glory above, is it not a poem, larger and more beautiful than any poet can compose?

What we feel, even if it were jubilant pleasure, is it more jubilant than all of the radiance and blossoming and fragrance here?

While I was thinking thus, a bird began to sing. I don't know what kind of bird it was. But its tones penetrated me and tore my heart upwards. And they think a bird when it sings has no feeling and no intelligence. His throat only an instrument. Who plays it? God? Who is God?

The vibrations of the ether, the rustling of the trees, of the sea, the whispering of the grasses, the thunder of the air merely a mechanical clanging back and forth? Not perhaps a language, an animated one? And we just don't understand it? Isn't it related to music? It too is wordless and can indeed be so deadly sweet, so eloquently enrapturing, and it can unsettle us to the point of annihilation.

The human creature is the least lovingly organized of all natural entities. Even the most sublime thought depends on a few little brain fibers. A little fiber tears. The thinker is an idiot.

But when wild vibrations rip up the heart of the Earth, when hurricanes tear through the air, nature remains the same. It heals the wounds that strike it and blossoms on and on, indestructible! Indestructible!

But do the great, earth-shaking ideas originate in the human brain?

Do they?

Or does the brain only receive them through mysterious fertilization? And the engendering—not possibly with transcendentally impregnated airwaves, spiritual whisperings, otherworldly messages?—From whom? From God? Who is God?

We are powerless. Stars tear themselves away, immense worlds, and stray as comets through the cosmos. Fire breaks out from the womb of the mountains, water out of the primitive depths of the Earth. Mountains rise above mountains. Primitive strength! Gigantic strength!

And I, I let myself be detained by fetters, thin as spider webs, in the belief that they would be untearable. A prisoner—in a backroom—in Berlin. I have to laugh at this idea! Loudly burst out laughing!

Sometimes I am angry that I am so soberly healthy. Only sickly people are clairvoyant, can see into the distance. Because the prison of the soul, the body, has become translucent? The fetters looser?

If only I were clairvoyant!

When I feel something deeply and mysteriously flowing in me, why do I not become clearly conscious of it, why can it not come to light?

I know, I know it, it is something in me that is more than I, that seeks the connection with the world soul (*Weltseele*). Connection with the glittering golden aroma above, connection with the gods there in the rosy ether, connection with———

Ach, it is not really true—what I have here so loosely fantasized, a lie. I am deceiving myself. I merely press forward into the distance, because I am so afraid of the narrowness of the four casket boards. I cling to the universe like a sheet anchor. It isn't true that I would like to quietly lose myself like the tone of a bell in the air, not true that I want to remain in Florence in a little house on the way to San Michele. I will never come back here. I do want to go farther—farther—always farther! Until I—the world soul—Also a phrase? Perhaps. Indeed, we know nothing! Only sparks! They die away—ashes!

∞

In Capri for eight days. I breathe only aroma. Nature is so full of goodness. Its tender air caresses a wrinkled cheek like a rosy one.

Wildly beautiful poetry, these ruins with their luxurious growing vegetation. A charmingly delightful work of nature atop the rotting, the decaying.

There are romantic, dream-like enchanted spots in Capri where nothing interrupts the loneliness except the soft blowing of the wind in the blooming bushes; it is so quiet that often the sudden flight of a bird frightens me. Unspeakable, unspeakable the sweet pathos of this softly resounding solitude. Wherever I turn, I am alone in a primeval forest of wild flowers. No rock from which weeds or flowers do not spring up. And in front of me, next to me, everywhere the sea, the blueness, a lacerating jewel on the breast of this landscape of lovely wildness, of tender grandiosity.

In the quiet, the sea appears more beautiful than the pale sky. The gentle flowing of the bluish silver sings rhythmically like the verses of Homer.

Even storms here are lovely. The blue waves with their silver little heads rage like tipsy Nereids. Their plaintive laments are long, drawn-out flute tones. Fantastically they ring up the cliffs. In the storm, only the stone-falcons shoot over the deep ultramarine of the water like announcers of a somber, mysterious message. A sounding, speaking, lamenting above the waters as if the riddle of the universe (*Welträtsel*) lay in its depth.

And how free one is here, free as the bird in the sky! No blocked off ways, no banks, no guards, no placard, no warning for the public. One sleeps nights with open doors. There are no criminals and thieves on this holy island. Everything wild, grow-ing, magically fairy-tale-like.

Neptune himself appears to have carried this island up out of the depths on his godly arms.

Is it also something godly here that carries my soul upwards?

Once, when I was still small, I saw a southern landscape with weathered columns, with cypresses and palms in a Berlin shopwindow, and ever since, when I went to the city, I always made a detour in order to see that picture. So irresistibly did it entice me.

Is this not inexplicable? Or does it explain itself so, that—

It happens that people who immigrated to foreign countries quite young gradually forgot their mother tongue. And after a half century perhaps, when they have a fever or are dying, they find it again, the language of their native land (*Heimat*).

Am I, too, feverish or dying, and will I find it here again, my native land? Was I merely thrown into Berlin to Philipp Street and to Steglitzer Street? Why then should I be there? Agnes Schmidt? Yes—but I?

∞

I love to walk through the streets and narrow alleys of Capri. They have an exotic appeal.

Every little house has a veranda and a pergola, decorated with columns, and around the columns hang vines that quite charmingly stand out from the whitish walls. Quaintly enchant-ing stairways. They lead upwards into empty air; they lead down-wards into holes; they cross, they intertwine; one doesn't see where they come from and where they lead to. Fairy-tale nooks in the narrow streets, a blackish piece of wall, in front of that a lemon tree, behind it the sea. And flowers! Flowers! Flowers in pots, flowers in dark containers. They grow out of the walls in wild tangles; they climb upwards on the moldy stone.

But there is one street that is only a long, narrow, vaulted, stony way, so narrow that two people can barely walk side by side. And it is dark in there and foul smelling. Garbage in every corner. And rooms open up onto these passageways, also stores in which edibles are offered for sale. Stairs lead up to verandas or to housing. These wall passageways have, as do tunnels, occasional openings through which the sea is blue and a pleasant sea breeze penetrates. And in these holes, people live, satisfied, happy, cheerful people; they don't see the terrible contrast between their aesthetic misery and the intoxicatingly poetic splendor around them.

Why am I astonished at that? I've indeed remained in intellectual misery my whole life, and not far from me were libraries full of intellectual treasures.

A half-weathered balcony in this dreary, stony street is decorated totally with sun flowers. I often see a small, rosy face peering out between the flowers onto the stone passageway.

In an open entryway, a pale girl sews a dress for the Virgin Mary. The naked, painted wooden figure with a child on its arm stands in front of her. And mother and child wear crowns. But, the pale girl coughs incessantly. And neither the heavenly queen nor the baby Jesus can help her, though they wear crowns. But they help her in another way—through her faith. This sick girl will die in the joyful hope that in the beyond she will sit to the right of the Mother of God, because she sewed the beautiful dress for her.

In its nakedness, the wooden figure is no object for her worship. It has to wear the clothes that she makes for it herself. Only then is it really a heavenly queen.

I've also worked and worked on sewing clothes for my heavenly king. And now I'm searching for the God to wear them, I'm searching for him—

❧

Often I wander amongst the ruins of Tiberius. At one place, the ruins appear to be a garden of stony grave mounds, on top of them, giant bouquets of yellow flowers. Yellow? No, gold. And only this one color, bewilderingly enticing. Flowers, as if conceived by the sun and born in ether. And everywhere, all around, the sea.

Further on, a small passage leads between two crumbling, low walls. The floor, a very old, Roman mosaic. On the low walls, an abundance of wild flowers; they burn in a rosy glow, they blaze in purple, and are abuzz and aflutter with bees and butterflies. The sepals on both sides of the wall touch up above and form a roof of flowers. Never have my lungs breathed a sweeter fragrance, never my eyes seen anything more charming. And here, here did Tiberius[8] throw his victims into the sea.

Is the human being really so much more than an animal? Even Tiberius? He, the beast of prey who mangled, and those whom he mangled were really also only lambs, indeed they let themselves be torn to pieces.

A gigantic lizard, shimmering in emerald-greenish luster, followed a butterfly. It rose to safety in the ether above.

Wings! Yes, wings!

One day we will also have wings. Whether real ones, whether only mechanically developed forces like wings—who knows!

∞

There are people here as beautiful and soul-stirring as the island. I have seen the man whom I would have had to have loved if I had met him in my younger years; a person whom nature created in an hour of meditation. I see him daily. When, for the first time, he crossed the threshold of the Hotel Pagano, he was dressed totally in white flannel and wore a passionflower in his buttonhole. His features are mild and noble, his eyes deep, crystal clear; one imagines seeing his thoughts glistening through them. He sits across from me at the dining table. He is like a psalm. I hear the sound of harps when he speaks. He is a doctor.

Someone asked him why he always wears passionflowers in his button hole.

"So many of them are blooming here," he answered, smiling.

I know better. He wears them because, as they say, the instrument of Christ's torture is symbolized in their flower cups. He wears them as a reminder, a kind of order of the cross, a sign that he belongs to a community that is still coming into being. Tolstoy is one of the masters of the order. He says it himself, his ideal is not that of the greatest living philosophers:[9] the "*Über-mensch*"; it is the "*Mitmensch*" (fellow-man). His religion is charity.

Recently, someone praised the devoted attention with which he cared for a sick child on Capri. He refused the praise—his charity is really only subtle egoism. "No one among us," he said, "would be able to eat, out of shame, while a starving person stood in front of him." Would it make a difference then if a single one of us, or thousands and many thousands stood behind us? Only because we don't see them? We still do know it.

How I would have loved him. But I have indeed loved him, if in my dreams, if in looking into my secret, inner self, I don't know. I loved him as a child when I looked in rapture at the moon; I loved him when the poetry that I read in school glowed through me. I loved him later when peculiar shudders rippled through my nerves while doing mechanical housework. It is an old love, as old as I myself am. He was preordained for me. And now we belong to different generations.

∞

When we have gotten up from the table, I hurry as fast as I can to the lonely heights of my favorite cliff. On the precipices beneath me are flowers and balsamic herbs, on every side the silver-bluish sea that sparkles in the sun and softly breaks on the cliffs. In the distance, the islands and peninsulas of the gulf.

I take off my hat, my gray hair blows in the wind. I stand straight and tall, my hands stretched upwards, and whether I recite verses, whether I only feel them, whether I compose them myself, whether it's the poetry of others—I often don't know. I pick whole hands full of wild flowers, and I let them fall on the path, one after the other. He takes the same path daily; he will step over the flowers.

They say that when a Roman hero and emperor set foot on Capri, a withered-up oak began again to flourish. So has—since he appeared—my heart also begun to flourish and blossom. Again? No, it is blossoming and flourishing for the first time!

Gray hair, creases, wrinkles! Am I this? No, no. I am in me, in me. I am only stuck in foreign skin.

> Odd that this skin is our fate.
> We have a smooth face. We love a person. Fine and good.
> A few wrinkles appear in our face. We love a person.
> Questionable.
> We have many wrinkles. We love a person. Ridiculous.
> Shameful.

Or does the peculiar lie in the fact that heart, mind, and skin do not dry up at the same time? Peculiar? Not natural perhaps? Because there is something in us that never withers, never dies, not even in death?

Is it my fault that treasures of love rest in my breast that were never elevated, and now the sun, that most blissful beauty, has brought it to light[?] A flood has come over my heart! Not love only for the one, but love for everyone, for everything, which, so flamingly persuasive, so full of the power of spring, overwhelms me.

I am indeed a new person. I am young. I have not yet lived. I must indeed be young.

I have the physical strength to transform myself. Like those mediums whom I have read about, who, when they quote the spirits of the dead, assume the voice and facial expression of the dead one in mysterious suggestion. Likewise I have quoted my dead youth. It is there, and my lips smile with the smile of young happiness, in my eyes is the light of youth. I am really and truly eighteen years old. I am bride-like. I have made my honeymoon trip to Capri, the blessed island, which is entirely a festive chamber for the wedding of two souls.

∽

On my solitary walks I came upon a cave that is called Matromania. This cave is wonderful with its powerful arches and blocks of stone. Inside, it has been developed like a temple, a remainder of old Roman masonry. A few steps are recognizable that lead to a sort of altar.

Here, Tiberius is said to have sacrificed a boy to the sun god. A very narrow opening leads into the cave. Through this opening, one looks out onto the sea. The effect from here is beautiful.

And Tiberius saw this flowing current of heart wrenching beauty, and it didn't subdue him, it didn't move him.

Suddenly it occurred to me how, if a small stone came loose from the arch and crushed me, or if it fell in front of the opening, I would have to starve to death in agony!

Yes, nature can be evil too, evil and cruel.

And perhaps it was this that made Tiberius so evil, so devilish. Daily he saw the fiery columns of Vesuvius, pregnant with devastation, flare upwards. He saw year for year how the sweet blue sea and the beautiful earth opened up and devoured living things with wild greed. Behind glistening magnificence, he saw death everywhere, everywhere. And this made him insane. And he spit his voluptuous, animalistic cruelness into nature's face like a gigantic mockery. "I am as powerful as you!" And in his wild death dances, he cried tears of fire.

That is why they also call the fiery wine here the "Tears of Tiberius."

It had become dusk. Dim glowing reflections of the setting sun fell into the deep darkness of the cave and dyed the drops leaking softly down red, red as blood. A shudder ran through me. My hands became ice-cold, and I had the hallucination as of a stone actually falling.

I sat there, shivering, without the strength to move. I thought I saw a golden bowl on the altar and in front of that an old man with a flowing, white beard. He touched the bowl with a staff, a whitish flame flared upwards, and out of the flame developed a jumble of dream-like beings, wildly fantastic things and lovely figures of light in gently colored veils with green wreaths on their wavy golden hair. Then it was a serious, beautiful woman, wrapped in black. And through all of this colorful fog, fiery butterflies whizzed. On the columns of the altar sat owls. Now a witches' Sabbath, then a fairy dream.

Through the black background of the cave ran a fiery quivering, a jubilant effervescence in every color, blue, red, green. And gradually, out of the spray, a rainbow developed, a beaming one, and it arched and swelled, crossways through the cave, forming a bridge that led into the open. And suddenly, the rainbow was a snake, a glistening, wonderfully lovely giant snake, and all of the chaotic figures swung themselves onto the living bridge and pushed outwards into the open. And I also climbed onto the bridge. Then the snake coiled around my body and pressed itself against my breast, and the snake spoke: "I am the sin, the sin of Tiberius. I am the bridge that leads to hell."

The last reflection of the sun had died away. The hallucination disappeared. I rushed out of the cave.

I think that a person is responsible for his dreams and hallucinations. Have I failed? With what? The man with the passion-flower—is he it? Is it because I also now still love him, even if in a peculiar way? With a sweet exaltation about the fact that I have found God in a person; as long as I am alone, I know that there is nothing in me that needs to shy away from the light. But as soon as I am among people, I see through the eyes of the others, think the thoughts of the others, then I feel I am guilty of a ridiculous anachronism, and I feel ashamed.

Sensuous love is only like the foam on a drink. When it has vanished, one enjoys the drink that much more purely. Sensuous desire often has nothing to do with the actual intellectual individuality of the desiring one, and what man and woman have in common here is only the excitability of the blood.

What a dark, peculiar idea—that love is there for the preservation of the human race like the gratification of hunger for the preservation of the body. The excitability of the blood exists for procreation, but not love, not love.

I love him, not as a mother loves her son, not as a sister her brother, not as a wife her husband. What I feel is freer, purer, an intimate, inspired camaraderie, born out of the deep-hearted yearning for being more, for recognizing more, for finding more, for looking further. The tender nestling of moods and thoughts into one another, yes they are also a tender voluptuousness, and the kisses that aren't placed upon the lips, but rather from soul to soul, they are an ecstasy too. An ardent thrill of the finest nerve filaments, particles that are sprayed from the world soul.

⚭

What I have written here about love, is this not bleak fantasizing and totally unrealistic? For others perhaps, not for me.

Most people would call the life that I have lived thoroughly realistic. For me it was only a pale phantom. The daily life that so mechanically occurs, what we eat, drink, and talk away about, physical love, all of this appears to me as shadowy, unreal. Undeniably, our body is realistic. But only our body?

They say a human being is half animal, half angel. Does the realistic only lie on the animal side? And what we inwardly live, what we see in half visions, what sings and sounds in the depth of our breast, in one word, everything that lies on the angelic side, this would not be realistic? But it fulfills me, it is my pain and my desire, my despair and my delight. And the love that I mean is just as realistic as the embrace of bodies.

And yet—yet. I am always afraid that someone could discover the secret of my youth and my love. Not he! Not he! Above all, not he! Recently, he passed by the place where I sat. He greeted, remained standing, he wanted to talk to me. I gave myself a decrepit look and turned away. Would he understand the double being within me? And that it isn't the old woman that loves him, rather the young girl who was eighteen years old thirty-five years ago?

No, I do not need to be ashamed of myself, the others have to be ashamed because they only understand what happens daily and what lies on the animal side and because they do not comprehend that it befits every age to shut that which is loveable into one's heart.

Even an old woman? The seventy-year-old Goethe loved a young girl because of her youth and her charm; and contemporaries and posterity admired in that Goethe's mental strength. But if an old woman feels deeply and strongly for a man because of his soul-beauty then she is—erotically insane.

Poor, old woman, don't let yourself, since you're still living, be sent to the realm of the dead. I love you, old woman. I know your intellectual toils. Indeed, I myself am old—old? Really? Or—

In my childhood, I read a story by Jean Paul[10] about an old person who, in tormented regret, despaired over his wasted life on New Year's Eve. And then he wakes up. It was only a dream. He is young. Life lies ahead of him. What if I too were really only dreaming that I were old? And I would wake up and would be young, and—

Ach yes! Ach yes! Again, I so often have the feeling of being suspended in the air, of flying as in the dreams of my childhood.

Yesterday, I again climbed up to the ruins of Tiberius. I found everything enveloped in fog, sky and sea were one. Light gray, impenetrable ether, only now and again a silver glint that immediately disappeared again. The blossoming, colorful bouquets down on the shore appeared to swim in the dreamy ethersea. Rustling tones over the abyss.

As the fog gradually retreated, the cliffs glittered in mystical brightness, in golden green, dark purple, faded brown. Here and there a reflection of the sun. Foam sprayed up. When I looked down into the twirling water for a long time, it appeared to take on form and gestalt. The surging foam became white bodies, out of the rays of light evolved golden hair. The sirens! And they waved and they tempted.

A hot melancholy made me cry. Too late, too late do I realize how beautiful the world is! How beautiful!

Now the sea gleams, now the wild myrtle blossoms for me for only a short moment. Lightning that flashes in this darkness—then night.

Soft, painfully thirsting melancholy envelops me, as the highest beauty inspires it, which grows beyond our heart and our head and which our organism is too inadequate to embrace ardently.

Too beautiful! Too beautiful! So soft and sweet and luxurious. I should not have come here. Florence had given me quiet and resignation, the North Sea strengthened my head and nerves. But here, everything is languishing, flattering caress, only blossoming and fragrance and dreams. The island of the sirens!

What was that? He threw a bunch of myrtles to me. I did see him. So a dream after all that I am old?—

I wound a wreath out of the myrtle, and I have set the wreath upon my head. Behind me, he departed. And yet I saw him as if he were walking in front of me, and as he distanced himself further, I continued to see him at the same nearness.

I saw him turn into the small wall passages that lead to the hotel. A young Capriote woman came towards him. How beautiful and graceful she was. He stood still—he—I touched the myrtle wreath. It fell to the ground. Now, he disappeared for me.

> On the way home, I was afraid of the water
> surface, of my reflection in it. I didn't want
> to lose the illusion.
> The illusion?
> But he did throw the myrtle into my lap!
> O you dearest person! You best of men,
> you know it! You know it! Revive me! Revive me!

∞

The ghost of Tiberius haunts! He lied! His countenance lies! The passionflower that he wears is a lie. I have torn it from his breast. The fragrance of Capri, the intoxicating fragrance, is poison. The blue sea—yes—a giant snake, a glittering, gleaming one! Sirens! My love—insanity! I want to drown it, drown it in the sea! Deep in the sea until it is dead—dead. The ghost of the Tiber!

∞

I didn't do it. Why make so much noise. Yes, it is in any case at an end. Be quiet! Quiet, old woman!

For a couple of days, I was two persons. Now I am alone again. Loneliness—the shroud of the superfluous.

The person in the casket who lifts the lid, lifts it a little, this is the image of our whole existence. The body—the casket. The burning desire, outwards—upwards! This is the power that wants to lift, wants to and cannot.

I was in Capri? No, in a desert. My lips burn, my blood burns—thirst—thirst!

∞

I have drunk from the wine, from the
   "Tears of Tiberius." I have drunk.
I am intoxicated with misery—intoxicated!

∞

Only quiet—only quiet! Away from here!
   Where to? It doesn't matter? What did I do to him?
Icy shudder—icy shudder! And this hammering
   here in my head—dull, dull and strong.
   That which shall burst!

∞

Poor woman! Poor woman! Miserable sex.
   You didn't think about that, an old woman
   with tears of passion in her eye—

∞

Sappho from the *Fliegende Blätter*.

An old woman with a heart that beats,
   with a brain that thinks –

Grandmother Psyche.

∞

Psyche, he said; he thus knows what sort I am?
   And yet—yet –
He too! He! So wise, so good, so fine! He too!
   If he cannot get beyond the thought patterns
   of his generation, then who can?
It is not my generation, not mine! I hate it!
   Hate it, this miserable epoch.
My head! My poor head! At the foot of the
   column, the blood-sprinkled one. Does it
   lie there? Or under the water above
   which the swans migrate? Why have they
   left me my heart! The heart! It must come

out, the twitching heart—bleeding one –
Why did I have to live as I—Didn't I already
write that once—and also about the bronze
tablets of law that—and about the casket—
and—one should shatter—shatter—my God—
How do you write that word? Shat—How
do you write—the lid!—Stop! Stop!—I—yes—ashes—

This is where the diary ends. Doctor Behrend did not find in it what he had hoped to find: psychological material for the origins of mental illness. Still, he was touched by deep human emotion as he now stepped to the bed of the dying woman. She sat upright. Her face was small like a shadow. She still wore the myrtle wreath. The sharp stems had become entwined in her hair. They had tried to remove the wreath and cut her in the process. A drop of blood ran over her forehead. Mechanically, she plucked the passionflower that lay on the cover to pieces. Her death-enchanted looks hung on the fiery ball of the setting sun. As she now spoke to the doctor, with a voice that was like echoing sounds of a harp, a tender smile played around her lips:

"An old woman who dies from the labor pains of birth. Will my "I" be born in death?—Will I in the Beyond become who I am?"

And after a pause, she began to speak again. Now her voice appeared to come from far away.

"I hear the swan song that the sun sings.
Red morning sky!"

With an expression of blessed listening, her head sank light as a breath back into the pillow. Without age, without sex was this dying countenance in which death and beauty were wed. The powerfully radiant eyes encircled by dark shadows appeared to traverse through Heaven and Earth throughout eternal times and infinite space.

They appeared to see and to understand what cannot be seen and understood on this side. In their light was a passing away and becoming, a dying off and a new life, an immeasurable sadness and an enthusiastic beholding full of exalted astonishment.

∞

Higher and higher climbed the pupils, until they gradually disappeared behind the wide eyelids.

∞

She lay there in death a marble statue of pure beauty, with a drop of blood on her forehead, the thorny myrtle on her head.

∞

The end

The Old Woman [1903]

Hedwig Dohm

Often, I have already fought for the rights of the woman, for the rights of the young girl, of the wife, of the mother. I have barely touched on the old woman here and there. I want to talk about her now; about the poor old woman who is like a shadow that creation—to the displeasure of humanity—casts. If the woman is or was generally—until a short while ago—the pariah of humankind, then the old woman was so threefold; and she still is it today. The young and younger—generations already born under happier constellations—simply haven't yet had time to get old.

I want to talk about the suffering of the old woman and tell how it is to be remedied.

That up to the present, woman has only been granted sexual worth has been said and lamented often enough. I will say it one more time, because this value judgment originates from the disregard to which the old woman is subjected. When a woman becomes incapable of being a bearer of and caretaker of children, or a lover, then her justification for existence has ceased.

All of the claims that, until now, she still was inclined to make on society seem more or less ridiculous; from those more mildly and more kindheartedly disposed, they are at least ignored.

Sexual appeal and utility as a measure of woman's worth! An animalistic interpretation of her being, a naïve shamelessness that may have been suitable for an earlier age, but that makes a mockery of the maturity and greatness of the present; for it dehumanizes woman. It is self-evident that in condemning this point of view, the sensuous and aesthetic joy of youth and beauty, the bliss of relishing love remains untouched.

There are funeral vaults for the living: lingering illness, incurable grief. Being old for a woman is also such a funeral vault. She is already interred in it during her lifetime.

Poor old woman! Everything gradually leaves you. In the beginning, your longing gaze follows those who leave you: children, friends, society; but they distance themselves further and further,—they disappear. Loneliness envelops you as if in a shroud, oblivion is the inscription above your house, the raven's song of hopelessness caws above your bed. Silence is around you; also you yourself are silent because no one wants to hear you. Poor old woman! You feel as if you have to be ashamed that you, now that you are so useless and already so old, are still living. Age weighs on you as guilt, as if you were usurping a place that belonged to others. Around you, you feel a sentiment that is pushing you out of this life.

A famous artist said to me once (as I was posing for him for a portrait, and I was over forty years old) that women who have lived longer than their fortieth year of life are a ballast for society and would do best if they would join their fathers [in death]. The earlier customs of barbaric peoples, who did away with superfluous female children immediately after birth, seem milder to me, since newborns—who are not yet familiar with the lovely habits of life—are likely to be less sensitive towards an accelerated advancement into the Beyond than much older adults.

I have heard good and well-meaning people say that old women are "something horrible." I heard this remark also from the mouth of a young woman who had a mother.

Here, I don't want to think about the dreadful tragedy—and it is not as seldom as one thinks—that arises when old women live too long for their relatives. In the educated classes, such cruel emotions are locked in the deepest depths of the heart. Contrarily, among the common folk, the pious wish that God would call away the old women is expressed openly often enough. The old woman—or also the old man—in the elderly phase—is tragic material that has found its treatment in literature. I'm thinking of *King Lear*, of Zola's *La Terre*, Turgenev's *A Lear of the Steppe*, of Balzac's *Le Père Goriot*.

Woe to the old woman who reads such a wish on a person's forehead. The delinquent, upon whose throat a wet cloth was flung at the execution site, died from imagining that it was the executioner's axe.

Nothing appears to me to be more paralyzing, more deadening for the old woman than the consciousness that is forced on her by society: you were, you are no longer. She shudders at this, as if she were hearing the clamoring bells that Death rings.

I know old women—sensitive characters—who prefer best of all living far from their relatives, in foreign cities, in foreign countries, out of instinctive fear of becoming a burden on their loved ones, like a sick animal that hides in the thicket of the woods.

I, however: I love you, you old women. I like to knock on the half-locked doors of your souls, and if they are opened to me, then I often experience lively hours which seem to me like evening prayers under silent stars. Some of you understand the voices that come from the graves; with others, one has the feeling (namely, when one is a theosophist) that their ethereal, their astral body has already partially freed itself from the prison in which the crude, material body had locked it up; it is as if, detached from the old home (*Heimat*), they were searching for a new one, one interwoven with a dark secret. That which happens around them in the nearest proximity, they only hear and see imperfectly. They see and hear into the remoteness, into the distance or deep within themselves. The gardens of the old [people] border on the Beyond.

One would think, when a woman has stopped being effective through her sexual appeal, that society would have to assess and appreciate her as a human being, according to her individual worth. This doesn't happen. The term "Old Woman" [*altes Weib*] includes a prejudice and precludes just appreciation. If mornings, a hunter first encounters an old woman, it means bad luck. Small children already learn to get the creeps from a witch, who is always an old, old witch. The devil is quite wicked. But, his grandmother rises to the height of wickedness. Ugh! The devil's grandmother! History is silent about the devil's mother.

> The overall feeling of society is against the old woman.
> I hear incensed calls: Oh! This certainly isn't true
>   for all of them!

No, there are exceptions. I knew some. They belonged to the stage or to the upper aristocracy. They were women who had collected treasures of experience in a rich, moving life; they were original women endowed with humor who had preserved their mental vigor and the ability to amuse into old age. To these exceptions also belong the aged women possessing inexpressible kindness of heart who create around us a lovely soft atmosphere that we breathe as violet fragrance. Fame, wealth, distinction are also mitigating conditions for "the old woman." However, these attributes must be present in great intensity in order to expiate the offense of age; their setting sun must illuminate the whole vicinity. Aside from these exceptions, up until now, the old woman has had meaning and influence only as wife or mother of a famous or high-ranking man. Would, for example, there ever have been a word passed on to posterity about "Frau Rat," despite her earthy, sparkling wit, if she had not been Goethe's mother?

⌒

The old woman casts her shadow beforehand in the matronly woman. One thinks of the matron with predilection as a picture of the mother-in-law, the old woman as the picture of the grandmother. I've already spoken about the mother-in-law. Here, I mention only that the mother, if she has a tenderly constructed soul, easily suffers from a mother-in-law consciousness even vis-à-vis her own married daughter; she must always be on guard so as not to interfere in the spheres of power and will of daughter and son-in-law, and to avoid rebuke. But, I want to talk about the grandmother.

For a long, long time already, the nursery has been empty for her, the realm in which she once practiced absolute ruler's rights, in which her heart celebrated orgies of delight and tenderness, where active caring and doing filled up her time and her thoughts.

Oh granny, granny [Großmütterlein]! Do you by chance want to creep into the nursery of your daughter? Stay out! You are no longer the ruler there, not even the vice-ruler; only a higher nanny with less authority than the actual nanny who holds her own through sternness and scolding while granny is branded as someone who is always frightened [Angstmeier].

Once, a five-year-old grandchild said to me as I scolded him because of a naughty deed: "But, grandmother, you don't matter here"! And he was a cute, sweet child.

And the essential thing is missing: the child's love. Grandchildren's love is an empty illusion, a luxury in the thrifty household of nature and only occurs as exceptions. The instinct of the child is against the old. And the love of the grandmother for the grandchild is also more a *Fautedemieux*-love, for want of other, more productive ones to cling to.

And if granny absolutely wants to be on the grandchild's good side, then she must curry favor through all sorts of feats, such as being the supplier of chocolates or toys. Caresses do not belong to this department.

By the way—let it be casually noted, the granny in the nursery of her daughter, as she exists in the imagination of the people as a frail old person, is a legend. She doesn't exist, or if so then only exceptionally, because when the grandchildren are still children in the nursery, the grandmother is neither old nor feeble, but rather, as a rule, still a vigorous, forcefully creative woman. My own mother still gave birth to two children after she already had three grandchildren. The tottering granny materializes only with adult grandchildren. The grandmother is confused with the great-grandmother.

The grandmother in the nursery of the daughter is a flowing source of conflict between mother and daughter.

And the reverence for age? This is preached all over and everywhere. Justly? No.

That which leads upwards to the heights, where temples stand in which gods live, demands reverence. However, that which is decaying, pointing backwards, doesn't demand reverence. The old may demand of us reverent sympathy, understanding for their needs, patience with their weaknesses, in isolated cases gratitude, but nothing more. Man certainly doesn't get old due to morals, in order to comply with a higher, ethical duty; he gets old automatically and gladly. And out of pure self love, even if he is already very old, he usually wants to get even older.

As the folk adage states: "Ninety years is child's mockery." Oh, the mockery already sets in earlier; it begins as soon as the weaknesses of age become noticeable, even if they are only weaknesses of memory or physical awkwardness. A good upbringing can keep utterances of sarcasm in check; it cannot replace it with reverence.

That presently more piety than respect is paid to age is undeniable. Perhaps this psychic (current) phenomenon is—at least partially—to be traced back to the following: In earlier epochs, the acquisition of learning and knowledge was only available to a small minority. The majority was dependant on that which trickled down to it through oral communication. The older, then, a person got, naturally, the more empirical knowledge was amassed by him; and the old thus became a source of knowledge from which the young generation drew and whose worth it honored with respect.

Now, today, all contents of knowledge are offered to everyone in such concentrated and also popular form, and they increase in all heights and depths so breathtakingly quickly, that the old almost always appear as outdated and no one needs them for intellectual enrichment any more.

And how does the salon, the social culture [*Geselligkeit*] conduct itself towards the old women?

Odd: if people did not always lie, even when everyone notices that they lie, then they would admit (verbally, they indeed do admit it, but on no account in print) that the old woman in the salon is unwelcome in society. As a rule, the hosts get embarrassed about where to seat her because the male guest, the older he is, the more forcefully he indeed reveals his antipathy towards the proximity of a woman of the same age; often he takes outright offence at this table arrangement. And seating the old woman next to a young gentleman—this is not the custom of the land.

I know an old, very lively and merry lady who immensely would love to go out in society. However, she declines every invitation. When asked about the reason for her refusal, she answered in her Silesian dialect: "*Man ist so ibrig*" [One is so superfluous].

Yes, she is right. The old woman is so "*ibrig.*" When a woman no longer comes into question as a sexual being, then her conversation is also no longer interesting. What she thinks, feels, opines is "*ibrig.*"

Socializing is by no means out of the question for the old man. If in advanced old age he is no longer forcefully creative, still through his knowledge, experience, through his social or political connections to the world, he still is rich enough to be able to take pleasure in himself and give it to others. And besides that, he has the tremendous advantage of not being an "old woman."

And does this disregard and setting aside of the old woman have no justification of any kind?

It has a justification, even if no reasonable person will agree with the brutal remarks of the famous doctor from Leipzig who describes the old woman as a monster. The justification lies in her superfluousness. This is indisputable if the contemporary social order relating to the old woman is validated as the only normal one for all of eternity. If the purpose of a woman's existence—as the majority assumes—is bearing children and raising children, then she has fulfilled her purpose when the children are grown. "The Moor has done his work, the Moor can go." In many cases, even another heightening of the superfluousness is allowed: she becomes burdensome when—as often happens—the old woman claims for herself considerations and attentions that impose sacrifice on her relatives, be it time, comfort, money. The old woman then no longer gives, she only takes.

To be sure: very few approach the inevitable human destiny of decaying into the highest old age. And since no one would sanction the folk custom of the old (East) Indians who dispatched their old ones to the realm of shades on the Ganges, then the family's helpfulness, and where none exists, then the state's, must assist the infirm old. One day, this help will be called upon by the helper of today when age has broken him. And therewith, a balance between giving and taking would be created.

With this burdensomeness, the financial question is of great weight. In the higher, educated classes, it happens that a young man cannot start his own family because he has to support or take care of female relatives. This financial duty weighs horribly on people. The employees who have to support the old mother from their meager wages do it with a heavy heart, almost always full of resentment and bitterness.

One day, I found my servant girl—a good, faithful creature—crying perplexed in the kitchen. In answer to my question, I learned that her mother (she lived in a small east Prussian village) undertook a trip in order to visit a married son whom she had not seen in many years. The trip cost fifteen marks. The girl was crying about these fifteen marks. She supported her mother with ten marks a month—half of her salary.

Among the general unpleasant attendant symptoms of age belongs the loss of beauty—if such did exist, which actually isn't as often the case as one tends to assume when contrasting youth and age. In the upper classes, the ugliness of age stands out more conspicuously in women than in men. Among the masses, with the farmers, the old man is no better looking than the old woman.

I remark here that the German old woman is generally uglier than the old English, American, or Norwegian woman. It is a disagreeable observation for German patriotic minds—one has the opportunity to make it in travel—how the interesting, character-filled heads, the slender, majestic figures of these female foreigners cast a shadow over the stockier, fatter German old ladies with their indistinct characteristics. I see the cause of this phenomenon less as a national or racial difference, but more as that in the above mentioned nations the house mothers (in the upper classes) are seldom women who, when the objects of their activities are taken away from them and the close circle of interest is scattered, easily become sluggish, dull, and fat. The intellectual essence calls forth the physiognomy. We read in the faces, as it were, between the lines; through all of the wrinkles shines the script that wrote a soul into the features. I repeat a quote that I already used once: "It is a justice on earth that faces become like people."

Age destroys the beauty of forms and lines. The effects of this destruction can be softened, in not rare cases neutralized. Old women tend to neglect their outer appearance, because they believe that it is totally inconsequential. They don't count any more. Who pays attention to them? Thus, at least, they take the easy way out.

They are wrong.

I would like for the old woman to dress herself in white. I think she is entitled to the color that is kindred to light. I would like to see something priestly, removed from the earthly, light-seeking in her. Not only does a barely still modern symbolism, but also so do aesthetic reasons speak for the white dress. No one more than the old woman should observe the rules of aesthetics. The most particular cleanliness and care in hygiene, in dress, should be her rule. Every kind of hygienic precaution and everything that serves the preservation of strength and flexibility, the avoidance of heaviness and corpulence belongs to the care of the body.

Objections will be made that the old woman provokes ridicule when she does things that aren't appropriate for her age. *Are* not appropriate, or not *considered* appropriate? This difference is important. Of that which is considered inappropriate, most is based on habit and contemporary prejudice. One proof of this is that an activity that makes an old woman look ridiculous, elicits approval—often very spirited—for a man of the same age. An old woman with ice skates on her feet, on a bike, on a horse: ridiculous; the eighty-year-old Moltke[1] on a horse was stared at in wonder as an admirable appearance; only benevolent looks follow the white-bearded ice skater.

My childhood still falls in the time when a female skater gave rise to astonishment and indignation. If, in my forty-fifth year, I would have worn a round hat with flowers, the youth on the street would have shouted after me. Today a forty-year-old wears the same hat as her daughter, and it is found to be in order.

On the advice of her doctor, due to congestion, a sixty-year-old lady of my acquaintance wanted to take up riding, naturally only on the track. She gave it up again, because she couldn't bear the joking and ridicule of her circle of acquaintances. Another old relative of mine was burning to hear the lecture of a certain university professor. She didn't have the courage to expose herself to the amazed looks of the young men.

Listen old woman, what another old woman says to you: Resist! Have the courage to live! Don't think for a moment about your age. You are sixty years old. You can reach seventy, eighty, even ninety. The youngest can climb into the grave before you. To think ahead about death, to feel it in advance, means rushing to meet it, means depriving the present. Even if you only live one more day, you still have a future ahead of you. Life is a struggle. Everyone says it. One fights against enemies. Age is an enemy. Fight!

Do whatever gives you pleasure, as far as your mental and physical strength lasts. Precisely because you do not have much more time left, exhaust every minute. The theosophical idea is of festive elegance: the richer of mind and heart we are when we climb into the grave, the more glorious our return will be.

Ridicule the ridicule by which you are intimidated, which wants to block the doors of pleasure for you. The child, as well as the old woman, has the right to life. Become, after all, old for the others: but not for yourself.

What do you old ones have to ask of society—that long ago dismissed you? Whoever does not want anything more of society no longer has anything more to fear from it. No one begrudges us the grave. You pussyfoots you! Why are you still listening to approval and hissing from this society?

If you have the inclination and the strength, then ride a bike, a horse, swim, discover new beauties, new worlds through travel. A seventy-six-year-old, famous English doctor tells of his long camel ride through the desert. Perhaps you can become as strong as this doctor and, as he did, ride through the deserts on camels. If you have it and are comfortable with it, let your white hair flow freely around your head. Mingle with those who are learning. It seems almost ridiculous to me that you feel ashamed to still strive for knowledge, as if death were a charmingly serious business that would be indecent to impede. A tree, even after it has given up all of its fruit, continues to live, resplendent in the new beauty of the autumn foliage until it dies from the winter frost.

I know a seventy-three-year-old woman who has begun to learn Latin; of course, she is receiving her lessons in a remote pavilion in her park so that no eavesdropper catches sight of this outrage. I know another: when she noticed that the words and expressions for what she wanted to say began to fail her, she didn't willingly allow her cranial nerves this slackening. As a child practices when learning to speak, so did she practice so as not to forget how. She recited monologues and lectures; she fettered her fleeing memory with fine art, replaced it partially with an exemplary order. She wrote a journal in order to give herself an account of her state of mind. And she achieved amazing results.

Do you, old woman, complain that people no longer wanted to know anything of you? And if mortals, usually all too mortal, no longer know of you: there is the transcendental. Bathe your soul in the moonlight of the spirits. Are only living beings the bringers of joy? There exists all of lovely and wild nature, with its secrets and manifestations. There are the animals. They know nothing about age and ugliness. They love you because of what you do for them. There are, above all, the dead. One often can converse better with them than with the living. They live for us through their works. The treasures of the mind and soul that they contain are inexhaustible. Therefore, do not speak of loneliness.

You were not taught the magic formulas with which these treasures are lifted? Yes: that's it.

The future will not need these pieces of advice that are meant for the present. If up until now the lot of the old woman resembled that of a person whose property has burned down and who is crouching on the grave of his possessions—does it have to remain this way? No. Limiting the needlessness of the aging and old woman to the set and insurmountable limits of nature will be one of the consequences of the women's movement. There are no measures one can take to prevent death; but there are many little measures against the early death of a woman. The strongest is: unconditional emancipation of woman and thereby the deliverance from the brutal superstition that her right to exist rests solely on her sex. Give a woman a richer content in life, practical or intellectual interests that rise above the immediate family, that, when she gets old, will incorporate her into the larger family of humanity and through the common ground of such interests connect her with general, social life. Let her be on her own instead of always depending on others. If the others are gone from her, she always remains superficial; and is (for) herself not superfluous.

Incessant activity, be it with hand or head, will—like oil for a machine—keep the strength of her nerves and brain elastic and will guarantee her mental longevity far beyond the years that until now meant the farewell from life for her. Inactivity is the sleeping potion that you, old woman, are offered. Do not drink it! Be something! Activity is joy. And joy is almost youth.

Afterword

I.

Hedwig Dohm was born in 1831, the third child and oldest daughter of eighteen children.[1] Her father was the factory owner Gustav Adolph Gotthold Schlesinger, who converted to Christianity in 1817 and changed his name to the less Jewish-sounding Schleh in 1851. He didn't marry her mother, Wilhelmine Henriette Jülich, until 1838.[2] Much of the information about Dohm's life comes from her own reminiscing in "Kindheitserinnerungen einer alten Berlinerin" [Childhood Memories of an Old Berlin Woman][3] as well as autobiographical hints that she gives readers in her novella *Werde, die du bist* and the novels *Sibilla Dalmar* and *Schicksale einer Seele* [The Fate of a Soul]. From these works, it is clear that Dohm had a troubled relationship with her mother. In her memoirs, she asserts that a bond between them was not established because her mother was unable to nurse her.[4] Her mother was also always busy with the younger siblings as well as with taking care of the large household; the quiet child Hedwig was easily overlooked. In addition, she was frightened by her mother's violent temper and even comments that child rearing and beating were almost identical. In contrast, Dohm's father never beat the children, but, at the same time, he knew nothing about them, nor they about him. Away at work, he was an absentee father, only a "Sunday papa" ("Kindheitserinnerungen," 66–67).

As a sensitive and intellectually curious child, Dohm resented the unequal treatment of sons and daughters. Daughters were given a much inferior education, which is exemplified by her claim that she never even learned correct orthography ("Kindheitserinnerungen," 70), something that Agnes Schmidt (*Werde*) also laments. Dohm also resented the physical limitations imposed upon girls. While boys were outside skating, playing, and being physically active, girls were supposed to sit still while doing handwork and mending ("Kindheitserinnerungen," 51–52). In contrast, she recognized how important physical activity is for a healthy body, mind, and soul—for both boys and girls.[5] Many of the (painful) memories of feelings and perceptions from childhood and adolescence subsequently were integrated into her fiction and provided a foundation for her theoretical writings as well.

Because of her active mind and her boredom with typical household work, she convinced her parents to let her attend a school for teacher training. In 1853, at age nineteen, however, Hedwig Schleh left this training school that she had just begun and "escaped" her mother and stifling family life by marrying Ernst Dohm (1819–1883), the chief editor of the humorist-satirical paper *Kladderadatsch*. Through him, she was exposed to political ideas and to literary-artisitic social circles. The Dohms' house became a meeting place for the intellectual elite of Berlin, including such personages as Ferdinand Lasalle, Franz Liszt, Fanny Lewald, Hans von Bülow, Alexander von Humboldt, Karl August Varnhagen, Theodor Fontane, and many other prominent figures of the time.[6] At first Hedwig was a more passive participant in these salon evenings because of her self doubts about her education (*Bildung*) and knowledge, but also because she and Ernst had five children in quick succession (one son [who died in 1866 at age twelve] and four daughters),[7] which kept Hedwig busy with managing the household and being a mother.

Little is actually known about her married life and her relationship to Ernst. Julia Meißner writes that Dohm's stubborn silence about her husband and their marriage leads to the assumption that their life together was not without problems, at least for Hedwig.[8] Dohm's granddaughter Hedda Korsch also comments: "Über Mimchens[9] Kindheit ist mir allerhand bekannt, nicht nur aus den autobiographischen Romanen, sondern auch aus Gesprächen. Mimchen erzählte oft und ausführlich über ihre unglückliche Kindheit" [I know quite a lot about "Mimchen's" childhood, not only from the autobiographical novels, but also from conversations. "Mimchen" talked often and exhaustively about her unhappy childhood].[10] However: "Über ihre Begegnung mit Ernst Dohm und über ihre spätere Beziehung zu ihm hat Mimchen nie mit mir gesprochen" ["Mimchen" never spoke with me about meeting Ernst Dohm and her later relationship with him] (20).

Although Dohm had dreamed of becoming a writer since childhood, her writing career did not really begin until 1867 with the publication of a two-volume history of Spanish literature, a work commission that she took over from her husband. But it wasn't until 1872 when her youngest daughter was older and she herself was forty-one-years-old that she published her first work about women's emancipation, *Was die Pastoren von den Frauen denken* [What the Pastors Think About Women]. Two more works quickly followed: *Der Jesuitismus im Hausstande. Ein Beitrag zur Frauenfrage* [Jesuitness in the Household. A Contribution to the Women's Question] (1873), and *Die wissenschaftliche Emancipation der Frau* [The Scientific Emancipation of the Woman] (1874). After these treatises, she experimented with theater, writing four social comedies between 1876 and 1879. Between 1890 and 1899, she wrote five works of fiction, including the novella *Werde, die du bist* (1894) and the novels *Sibilla Dalmar* (1896) and *Schick-sale einer Seele* (1899), two parts of her trilogy (the third part, *Christa Ruland* was published in 1902). Thereafter, her fiction is interspersed with theoretical works. Shortly before her death, she wrote her last article: "Auf dem Sterbebett (1919, nach dem Weltkrieg von 1914–1918)" [On Death's Bed (1919, After the World War of 1914–1918)].[11]

In the course of her long life, Hedwig Dohm saw and experienced many events that undoubtedly shaped her as a person, writer, and thinker. One historical occurrence in particular that influenced her was the Revolution of 1848. Her granddaughter Hedda Korsch writes that Dohm had often told her about the incidents of that year and claims that Dohm viewed this experience as a turning point in her life, a claim substantiated by Dohm's inclusion of the 1848 Revolution in her autobiographical work. Although her parents had forbidden her and her younger siblings to go out once the unrest broke out in the streets of Berlin, Hedwig went anyway and saw armed troops shoot into a group of students. One of the wounded died right at her feet. Korsch writes that from this moment on, her grandmother was an enemy of all armed violence and a comrade of all freedom fighting ("Erinnerungen," 21–22).

Dohm's sense of social justice was thus awakened early on, and the burgeoning women's movement (the first wave of feminism) of the nineteenth century provided an ideal venue for her lifelong commitment to fighting for freedom and equality. And, finally, just before her death in June 1919, she was able to see some success for all of her efforts on behalf of the women's movement with the passage of women's suffrage (November 1918),[12] a right for which she had been an untiring champion for so many years and which she had so radically advocated in her essays and pamphlets on women's emancipation, even while other women's rights activists refused to support suffrage. However, Hedwig Dohm was not a champion for women's rights only. Her democratic vision included improving life for children and the poor and being a committed pacifist; she was one of few Germans or Austrians who did not jump on the bandwagon of World War I. She believed that equal rights for women were a key component in making life more humane for everyone, as is expressed in a quote from her 1876 work, *Der Frauen Natur und Recht* [Women's Nature and Privilege], that Heike Brandt uses as the title of her biography on Dohm: "*Die Menschenrechte haben kein Geschlecht*" [Human Rights Have No Gender].[13]

She was indeed concerned about human rights, and that her argumentation focused on the plight of women was a reflection of her society and times—that half of the human population suffered injustice and inequality solely on the basis of gender.

II.

Dohm wrote *Werde, die du bist* in 1894 at the age of sixty-three. In it, she touches on many of the same issues that concern her throughout her work: familial and marital relationships, women's position in society and in the home, and aging (particularly for women and especially for widows). These topics are also the focus of her essay "Die alte Frau," written nine years later. Dohm's open discussion in these works, and in her writing generally, about the sociocultural, psychological, and financial problems that aging presents for women, demonstrates her courage and just how forward thinking she was, as this topic was not socially acceptable (as made clear in the two works)—and is a topic that still today is widely ignored.

On the surface, the title of the novella is an imperative: *Become Who You Are*! As the Enlightenment philosopher Immanuel Kant appealed to man to have the courage to know and use his own reason (*Sapere aude*! was his motto), so does Dohm call for women to become who they are, which presupposes a search for identity and self-knowledge. However, besides this obvious appeal to women's reason, the title playfully makes reference to literary predecessors: the Greek poet Pindar, Goethe, and Nietzsche. In her study on Dohm's prose works, *Schreibe, die du bist* [Write Who You Are],[14] Gaby Pailer documents the degree of intertextuality that Dohm incorporates into the title and, further, points out the deconstructive aspect of Dohm's use and modification of this phrase.[15] "The Old Woman" is an essayistic substantiation of the fictional call for women to acknowledge their self-worth, to follow their instincts, and to "become who they are." It also presents an overt reproach of society for ingrained social habits and customs that repress, limit, and imprison older and elderly women while keeping them dependent and at the same time resenting them. The following discussion presents a short summary of and commentary on the action of the fictional novella within the context of Dohm's nonfictional appeal for rights for the aging.

∞

Werde, die du bist is a frame story that opens in the mental hospital of Dr. Behrend in Berlin. The sixty-year-old protagonist, Agnes Schmidt, has been in the hospital for about two years, and because of her age, she is viewed as old by society. The narrator tells us that she has a rather eccentric appearance, but her behavior is usually quite taciturn. One Sunday, on her sixtieth birthday, a young doctor friend of Behrend visits, and Agnes Schmidt, who recognizes the visitor, reaches out for him, and calls him her fiancé, and addresses him as Johannes, saying that she knew he would come for her. Dr. Behrend grabs the "madwoman" and firmly tells her to come to her senses, for she is an old lady! She then falls unconscious. In apologizing to his guest, Dr. Behrend assures him that she had never before had such an attack of erotic insanity. However, the young doctor admits to Behrend that Agnes Schmidt did indeed recognize him from Capri from years earlier and also that his name is Johannes. He tells Behrend what little he knows about her from that encounter, which offers a foreshadowing of what the reader will learn from the inner story. Dohm quite poignantly addresses the inherent cultural discrepancy that allows older and even elderly men to fall in love and have erotic relationships with (much) younger women, whereas for women, such an occurrence is cause for distain. In "The Old Woman," she points out just how pervasive this attitude is in society on all levels. Old, white-haired men are admired for their erotic activity and physical deeds or intellectual pursuits, while old, white-haired women feel compelled to hide their activities or pursuits for fear of ridicule. In *Become,* Agnes Schmidt's personal story exemplifies these discrepancies quite clearly.

After she regains consciousness, it is obvious that she also totally has regained her clarity of mind, and she gives Dr. Behrend the journal that she had begun at age fifty-four, two years after her husband died, so that he can discover how and why her mind became disturbed. The inner story, and by far the bulk of the novella, is made up of these diary entries that clearly document a search for identity. Who am I? What am I? are fundamental questions that Agnes Schmidt grapples with in her quest for a self, for her self.

Outwardly, Agnes Schmidt has been first and foremost a wife and mother. As Dr. Behrend's inquiries establish, "everyone [. . .] agreed that she had been a good, well-mannered, somewhat limited and philistine housewife, ignorant and totally absorbed with family life" (2). In her diary entries, she only briefly reflects on her life prior to the present (*Erzählzeit*), though the limitations and conformity imposed on her (because of her sex) and that have shaped her are essential questions of identity with which she struggles. After a relatively unhappy childhood, a reflection of Dohm's own childhood experiences, she married the Privy Councilor Eduard Schmidt and became a devoted mother of two daughters. Ever since her youth, she liked to read and was disappointed that as a young girl she was kept so busy with mindless handwork and household chores and, later, with the managing of her own household that she had no time to read. Her consolation for putting off her own needs and wants was that she and Eduard would travel once their daughters were married. However, shortly after the daughters' marriages, Eduard became ill and required constant care the last eight years of his life, care that he permitted only Agnes to give to him.

On the surface, Agnes Schmidt appears to have led a traditional life. She is and has done nothing which society would view as out of the ordinary: being a devoted wife and mother, dedicating herself to others, and selflessly taking care of them had been expected of her. Once Agnes Schmidt is widowed and left alone, she seeks rest after the hard work of the past few years, yet rest does not come, and she writes: "And now it started, quite gradually—the strangeness, the gnawing, the ruminating, the frightfulness" (15). At first she identifies this restlessness and her feelings as madness, an interesting conclusion, seen from our twenty-first-century perspective, but one that reflects the prevalent thinking of the time.[16] She must be mad because of what she found herself feeling and thinking. Though, when she thought back on her life, she realized that she had felt similar sensations periodically, most notably when she was sitting at her sewing machine, a tedious, female activity that she had always resented and that had always stifled her. She realized that she felt estranged by this activity, which can be traced to her (and Dohm's) resentment about the activities that girls were forced to pursue (handwork, sewing), or not allowed to pursue (playing and outdoor activities). But now, she is able to or can allow herself to think about these unfamiliar feelings. She starts to question the roles she has occupied in life, first as daughter, then as wife and mother, and then as mother-in-law and grandmother. She finally has the opportunity and the time to pursue reading—that forbidden passion from childhood. Now she has the sense of already having had some of the thoughts that she finds in the books she reads (25). This leitmotif recurs throughout the novella and contrasts with the fact that she had been a maid her whole life, as she comments (25). Books not only make her aware of an inner life she has been repressing, but they also expand her knowledge, her awareness of new ideas, and they introduce her to current authors and new belief systems. In addition, they represent an escape from the limitations that have confined her. These ideas are also present throughout "The Old Woman," when Dohm encourages woman to educate herself, to pursue her intellectual interests, and to resist the social constraints that repress her.

For Agnes Schmidt, her journal entries most fundamentally reflect and record her (lack of) sense of self and her search for an identity within the constricted context of a widowed, aging woman—the same "old" woman whom Dohm tries to awaken and motivate in her essay. Though Agnes Schmidt's inner story, in a double sense—her *inner* life as well as the *inner* frame story—, is told in the first person, the reader is nonetheless presented with at least three different perspectives about widowhood and aging, roles of women in general, and the meaning of identity: a societal, a familial, and a personal perspective.

Social norms and familial attitudes are incorporated into the novella mainly through Agnes Schmidt's reactions to them. It was expected that she would go and stay with her daughters and their families soon after the death of her husband. She kept finding reasons not to do so, most of which had to do with feeling intimidated and misunderstood by them. Yet, finally, she decides to go and even hopes that she will be able to talk to Magdelene about her "shattered nerves" (18). Once at her daughters', however, she feels disconnected from them, unneeded, unwanted, and generally superfluous. She thus conjectures: "Maybe children are indeed only an episode in a woman's life, and they quit being daughters when they have become mothers. It is almost an anachronism that they still have a mother. Also, they live in another time, in another circle. That's why a mother is out of place at her children's" (24).

In "The Old Woman," as well as in her longer polemic work, *Die Mütter*,[17] she substantiates this opinion, stating that children gradually become distant because ascending and descending paths don't meet. Daughters who have become mothers stop being daughters (*Mütter*, 184). In addition, she is the brunt of her sons-in-law's jokes[18] and feels that even her small grandchildren do not take her seriously, a point that Dohm reiterates in "Old Woman" about an incident with her own grandchild (71). Yet, at the same time, Agnes Schmidt thinks that the family couldn't purposely be treating her this way, and so her discomfort and angst make her paranoid. She recognizes that had she tried to talk to them about her nervous state, they would have thought she was losing her sanity, which portends the end of her story and of her life.

After she gets back home to Berlin and is on her own, she is no longer as if numbed (24) and even becomes courageous enough to venture out on long walks and go to the theater and galleries. And she reads. She becomes exposed to a world that had always been close but never available to her, and she longs to travel, which concretely represents escape from the routine of her daily life. Yet, she also is exposed to social prejudice, as her Sunday adventure to a suburb of Berlin revealed, for example, when she happened on a *Volksfest* and, as an old woman, became the brunt of young ridicule—again the motif of old versus young, particularly for women. Still, she has the sense that her chained-up nature has been released—which reflects Dohm's call in "Old Woman" for resistance to accepting and acquiescing to social constrictions.

Interspersed with the excitement of new discoveries, as the "Old Woman" encourages, Agnes Schmidt also records her thoughts on growing old in this society, her doubts, her questions; she even writes about the process of writing, which seems to come naturally for her (37). Then, unexpectedly, she inherits money from a relative and vacillates between what she views as her motherly duty—giving the money to her struggling son-in-law—or pursuing her lifelong dream of traveling. She decides to travel, first to the North Sea, then to Italy—reflecting the classical goal of a well-rounded education (*Bildung*) for nineteenth-century male writers, artists, and intellectuals. This also accentuates Dohm's incorporation of the (male) German literary tradition in the work.

Agnes Schmidt's adventures in travel and reading mirror as well as parallel her inner exploration. In the beginning, she lacks a sense of self, which is clear from her comment that no one can like her (20), or when she realizes that her only identity up until her husband's death was as his wife—and now as his widow. She has and has had no life of her own on her own terms. She notes, ironically, that the Indian widow-burning tradition has a deep meaning "—still today, and not only in India" (20). It makes most sense since society identifies a woman only in the context of her husband (and family). Indeed, on her deathbed, she tells Dr. Behrend: "I don't want to be buried [...] Burned, in flames blazing upwardly—in flames! That I want" (8). In "The Old Woman," Dohm reiterates just how intertwined a woman's identity is with that of her husband's. And in the context of aging, she further notes the East Indian ritual of ridding society of dependent elderly by dispatching them to the "realm of shades on the Ganges" (74).

Two metaphors embody particularly well Agnes Schmidt's state of mind in her pursuit of her quest. The first is a statue that is missing its head that she comes across while she is on a walk in the zoological gardens of Berlin. She subsequently identifies with the headless statue, and the sensation of having a loosely attached head recurs throughout the novella. The other metaphor is a painting she had seen on a visit to a gallery of a living person trapped in a casket who desperately is trying to lift the cover and escape.[19] As Pailer points out, Dohm takes up this metaphor as a motif in her works, especially in *Become*, to signify women who are similarly imprisoned (in the caskets) of the dominant view of womanhood (Pailer, 4).

Agnes Schmidt has numerous visions and hallucinations throughout the novella, an indication of her (distraught) state of mind. However, these visions also allow her to envision or imagine other ways of being, living, and thinking, underpinning the central question: who/what am I? Up until recently, she had been just her husband's wife. Now, visions of the possibilities of a different, of a missed life make her wonder who she is, really. On the one hand, she comes to view herself as a "thing" begun that won't be finished (39), a work in progress; on the other, she talks about the murder of the [her] soul and realizes that no one in particular has committed this murder, only that she was born a hundred years too early (42). Thus, she recognizes how deadly social confines—the casket lids—are for women, and also foresees a future time when this will have changed. This future will also be a time when humans will have wings. The image of flying, of having wings, underscores the yearning for boundless (bodiless) freedom (43).

As her search progresses, she becomes ever more estranged from the image of herself in her prior life and the role she occupied: "But I wasn't even an 'I.' Agnes Schmidt! A name! A hand! A foot, a body! No soul, no brain. I have lived a life in which I wasn't even present" (33). Later, the protagonist ultimately asks: what do Agnes Schmidt and I have in common? (40). Agnes Schmidt fulfilled the role of the docile housewife perfectly and unquestioningly, whereas "I" embraces the chaos of the visions and hallucinations and inner confusion that are part of her quest. While on her journey in Italy, this new and amorphous "I" discovers love. Within the context of aging, Agnes Schmidt dramatically embodies the inner dilemma of a young heart and soul trapped within the body of an old woman. She is aware of even being able to take on a young appearance because she feels so youthful. Yet, because she knows that this is not society's view, she purposely adopts and exaggerates the aura of an old woman, the old woman that society chooses to see. The ambiguity is so acute that even the young doctor (Johannes) notices it, as he tells Dr. Behrend in the frame story. Indeed, it is her perception about who this young man is that awakens love (and youth) within her. She realizes that love is transcendent and humane and not only physical, as she records in her diary:

> I love him, not as a mother loves her son, not as a sister her brother, not as a wife her husband. What I feel is freer, purer, an intimate, inspired camaraderie, born out of the deep-hearted yearning for being more, for recognizing more, for finding more, for looking further. The tender nestling of moods and thoughts into one another, yes they are also a tender volup-tuousness, and the kisses that aren't placed upon the lips, but rather from soul to soul, they are an ecstasy too. (60)

She feels a soulful, an intellectual kinship with him; yet, she does wonder whether he would understand the double being that she is—the young girl of long ago buried *within* the body of an old woman.

She is not ashamed of herself for these thoughts and feelings, but rather thinks that the others have to be ashamed for their lack of understanding that "it befits every age to shut that which is loveable into one's heart" (61). Further, she comments that "as long as I am alone, I know that there is nothing in me that needs to shy away from the light. But as soon as I am among people, I see through the eyes of the others, think the thoughts of the others, then I feel I am guilty of a ridiculous anachronism, and I feel ashamed" (59–60). She is torn between her inner truth and an outer social reality. Society would understand the love that an older man has for a younger woman, but that of an older woman for a younger man would be perceived as ludicrous: "The seventy-year-old Goethe loved a young girl because of her youth and her charm; and contemporaries and posterity admired in that Goethe's mental strength. But if an old woman feels deeply and

strongly for a man because of his soul-beauty then she is—erotically insane" (61). Her double identity is again made clear to her:
the outwardly, physically old woman versus the inwardly youthful
"I." The young doctor perceptively recognizes Agnes Schmidt's
youthful core and one day even throws flowers at her feet when
he sees her (in a youthful mode) at the cliffs by the ocean. This
incident confirms for her that he *is* special and that they have a
soul connection; yet later she overhears her idealized Johannes
making fun of her (Grandmother Psyche) with another guest
(who ridicules her as Sappho from the *Fliegende Blätter*), she not
only is acutely reminded of the societal limitations imposed on
her and of being misunderstood and appearing ridiculous to
others, but the episode also signals the end of her journal and
presumably propels her into a state of "madness," since she subsequently ends up in Dr. Behrend's sanitarium.

The image of Agnes Schmidt in the end—in the frame
story, after Dr. Behrend has read her journal—has biblical over-
tones. She wears the myrtle wreath (which Behrend assumed rep-
resented a bridal wreath) on her head, but now, dried up and
thorny, it underscores her role as a Christ figure, as a sacrificial
lamb, particularly with the droplets of blood that are on her forehead. Moreover, she overtly evokes this Christ imagery by asking
Behrend: "Many women die on the cross, but whether only to be
dead, like the poor thief, or whether for others, like our Savior?
... Yes for the others—the other women" (8). As a Christ figure,
she is willing to die to help others. Unlike Christ, the blood on
her forehead comes from the staff trying to remove her "crown of
thorns," whereas Christ received his wounds when the "crown"
was placed upon his head.

It appears that Agnes Schmidt ultimately submits to the
societal demands placed on "old" women by becoming "insane."
At the same time, however, one could question the socially
imposed perspective that she is (must be) mad and argue that she
seeks out the sanitarium as a refuge and solace, as the only place

where she can continue to pursue her inner life; where she can continue the search for an (inner) identity, where she can continue to dream about and envision a more fulfilling life—one filled with self-determination, self-awareness, and with opportunity (for women). On her deathbed she thanks Dr. Behrend for his care and interest: "Here in your sanitarium, I was less insane than during my whole, previous life. I had great thoughts, saw wonderful things. Dreams and visions are indeed also life" (7). This was often the only possibility for nineteenth-century women.

It seems that Agnes Schmidt has found her identity in her "madness." Ironically, her confinement in the "insane asylum" is a time of opportunity for self-exploration and inward self-determination. And, just as her experiences in the sanitarium are full of ambiguity, so is her death. As she is dying, her death seems to represent resignation or succumbing to an outwardly imposed destiny. Most concretely, death implies failure, because it is the physical end. Such an ending seems diametrically opposed to the adamant appeal that Dohm presents to women in her essay. However, it is Agnes Schmidt's apparent resignation, representative of generations of female thought, that lies beneath and motivates Dohm's resounding call for change, for resistance. At the same time, Agnes Schmidt triumphs in her death, because she dies as a self-aware, self-confident, and enlightened woman, that is, human being. This, again paradoxically, undermines the societal restrictions placed on women as well as the basic concept of death.

III.

Writing, producing text, allows Agnes Schmidt to explore her "self," to try and discover as well as assert an "old woman" identity. She processes her emotions and thoughts by recording them in journal form, and in turn, writing constitutes a process for her that (also) reflects, at least an effort at, self-revelation. It also is symptomatic of her situation—she cannot *talk,* thus she writes. The title of Gaby Pailer's book on Dohm signifies the importance of this process: *Schreibe, die du bist*. At the same time, it is an imperative (as is Dohm's title) that calls for the searching woman to textualize and thereby realize her identity. The genre of the diary or journal necessarily is fragmentary; it is stream of consciousness (reminiscent of many prolific and well-known male authors,[20] who wrote around the same time); it is full of ellipses and (as Dohm often remarked and as Agnes Schmidt lamented) incorrect orthography. On the one hand, this underscores the frequent lack of formal education for females that Dohm repeatedly addresses in her works; on the other, it realistically mirrors the style of the genre—a genre that has been open to women writers while others have been much less accessible to them.[21]

Two main criticisms recur in critical studies about Dohm's fiction writing: first, questions about the quality of the writing, and second, the lack of political activism so clearly dominant in her nonfiction works. Elisabeth Plessen writes, for example, that the directness, the freshness, the heretical humor, the erotic play with language that all typify her polemics are all missing in her fiction.[22] These two lines of reasoning are most often delineated by sociopolitical or activist views of feminist criticism; thus, as Pailer points out in Dohm's case, her fictional work is (most often) viewed in comparison with her polemic works (10). However, Pailer remarks that the nature of the genres in question has to be taken into consideration: the differences between fiction and polemic writings. She also notes that, within this context: "...Dohm [zeigt] nicht weniger Witz und Spiel mit Sprache als die polemischen Texte: nur handelt es sich eben um literarischen Witz und um gestaltetes Spiel" [Dohm doesn't show less wit and playfulness with language as in the polemic texts: only that it's all about literary wit and about designed playfulness] (10).

Certainly the witty use of language and her playfulness can be noted in the intertextuality evident in her works, specifically these two texts. In reference to Goethe, for example, Agnes

Schmidt ironically compares herself to an old Mignon, or she directly evokes Goethe—as an older person (man) who would be viewed differently than she, the old woman. In the essay, Dohm further remarks just how important it is that Goethe is Frau Rat's son in order for her wit even to be recognized and acknowledged.

Biblical references are also frequent. Besides the image of Christ at the end of the work, invoking the New Testament, there is also the image of Moses receiving the Ten Commandments (governing religious and social law) from God on Mount Sinai from the Old Testament. Agnes Schmidt questions the belief that social customs are written onto (Moses's) tablets of stone; are (any) laws, just because written on ancient stone, still valid? She questions the signifiers that socially have determined her life and wants to shatter the stone tablets. Aptly, this image concludes her diary entries and signals the disintegration of her ability to write—she is only able, in writing, to stammer partial words that she had previously written. This also marks the onslaught of her "insanity" and signifies her realization that not only is she in actuality (*tatsächlich*) a ludicrous (societal) anachronism, but also that her quest is futile, at least as seen or judged by others, by social law, as is so well documented in "The Old Woman."

While Dohm's nonfiction texts directly and very systematically and vehemently address arguments that male thinkers of her time held fast, this does not mean that her fiction ignores these dominant social "ideals." Ruth-Ellen B. Joeres maintains that Dohm's works are ambiguous;[23] there are often, for example, moments of optimism in her polemics; yet her fiction is dominated by pessimistic images ("Zähmung," 218). She further observes that critics writing about Dohm's narrative works note that the (female) protagonist appears insecure and unclear.[24] However, she also writes that both genres complement each other. Indeed, for a more complete perspective on the author Dohm, one needs to examine all genres in which Dohm wrote; yet, her feminist strategy and emancipatory concerns are clearly evident in the fictional text *Become,* and the juxtaposition here of a novella and an essay, both of which deal with the aging process and assertion of identity for women, clearly illustrates this complementary relationship. Dohm's fiction may present a more pessimistic view than she typically presents in her nonfiction, as Joeres states; nevertheless, she realistically portrays the male-dominated culture within which women lived in the last quarter of the nineteenth century. Although Dohm does not specifically discuss the women's movement or political activism in this novella, she does address issues that dominated feminist thought of the time: for example, when Agnes Schmidt visits her daughters and brings up such topics as education for girls,[25] or women in medicine during evening discussions. But she is then immediately ridiculed by her son-in-law (20–21). Later, she writes that she is convinced that a mother's enlightened good sense is best for children's education, a topic that Dohm also touches on briefly in "Old Woman" and addresses more thoroughly in *Die Mütter.*[26] The lack of education (*Bildung*) for girls and women is an important aspect of Dohm's fiction and nonfiction alike and was not only a dominant topic for Dohm, but generally for women writers of the late nineteenth century. In *Become,* Agnes Schmidt repeatedly bemoans not only her lack of education but also her desire (and current striving) for edification and knowledge—which exemplifies the issues that determined and preoccupied the first women's movement.

Of course, the main emancipatory aspect of the novella is the persistent, if sometimes insecure—though for this reason, realistic—search that the protagonist undertakes. And Dohm presents this quest very persuasively, juxtaposed against the patriarchal society within which she and within which Agnes Schmidt lived. "The Old Woman," on the other hand, boldly calls for open rebellion, resistance, and the overthrowing of social norms, which Agnes Schmidt could only envision for the future.

Moreover, although Dohm wittily and purposely incorporates (male) literary "greats" into her novella (into her works in general), she specifically uses a "female" language and thought processes as an underlying, a feminist strategy.

IV.

"Become who you are" is not only a reference to and a play on Pindar, Goethe, and Nietzsche, or even an appeal for enlightenment à la Kant; it also can be viewed as Dohm's motto or as a slogan for nineteenth-century women in general. Clearly this novella is a provocation not only for Dohm's contemporaries, but also for women of all ages. It presents, perhaps, a more subtle call for change than is obvious in her essay, yet the provocation is evident.

In this work, Dohm questions the assumption that women are caretakers only. Agnes Schmidt has devotedly carried out her duties as a wife and mother (a role that many women, even now, assume) to such an extent that she ignored her own needs, to the detriment of her self. Thus, the novella records the protagonist's effort to discover an "I"—which, as Ute Speck argues, is a social construction.[27] Perhaps any "I" in any age that we are able to partially dis- or uncover is a social construct, considering the norms and delineations that we internalize from our family situation, from the period (age) in which we live, and from the literary tradition/s to which we are exposed. Within this context, Agnes Schmidt "heroically" pursues her quest—in the manner that Dohm outlines in her nonfiction.

Finally, I would like to note that after her long and arduous search (for self), Agnes Schmidt comes to the conclusion that she "will become nothing" (39) ("ich werde nichts [56]). Though this can be (and often has been) viewed as failure, that it is not in the least unexpected, given her background and the sociohistorical context from which she comes. Much more disturbing is Dr. Behrend's inability to understand what her diary entries document—and mean. He, like she, is caught up in the patriarchal thinking of the time, despite his expertise as a psychologist. At least he leaves her in peace—and has allowed her the freedom to pursue her "madness."

Though both of these texts were written over a century ago, they speak to contemporary women with their poignancy and, on many levels, up-to-datedness. Dohm's perceptiveness is to be thoroughly admired, particularly since—though many aspects of life have improved for women—many of her observations and insights about the search for self still ring true today for women, as her concluding remarks in "Old Woman" suitably illustrate:

> Give a woman a richer content in life, practical or intellectual interests that rise above the immediate family, that, when she gets old, will incorporate her into the larger family of humanity and through the common ground of such interests connect her with general, social life. [. . .] Incessant activity, be it with hand or head, will—like oil for a machine—keep the strength of her nerves and brain elastic and will guarantee her mental longevity [. . .]. Inactivity is the sleeping potion that you, old woman, are offered. Do not drink it! Be something! Activity is joy. And joy is almost youth. (79)

Notes

Preface

1. Much has been written about this phenomenon, but the titles of Luise F. Pusch's (editor) books perhaps most clearly illustrate it: *Mütter berühmter Männer. Zwölf biographische Portraits* (Frankfurt am Main: Insel, 1994). Among women included in this text are Katharina Kepler, Dorothea Händel, Maria Anna Mozart, Johanna Schopenhauer, Betty Heine, and Franziska Nietzsche. *Töchter berühmter Männer. Neun biographische Portraits* (Frankfurt am Main: Insel, 1988). Daughters in this work include the daughters of Achim von Arnim (Gisela), Karl Marx (Eleanor), Theodor Fontane (Mete), and the daughters of Johann Sebastian Bach. *Schwestern berühmter Männer. Zwölf biographische Portraits* (Frankfurt am Main: Insel, 1985). Among the sisters included here are Cornelia Goethe, Maria Anna Mozart, Ulrike von Kleist, Luise Büchner, Elisabeth Förster-Nietzsche, and Carla Mann.

2. *Werde, die du bist* was published with another of her novellas: *Wie Frauen werden. Werde, die Du bist. Novellen* (Breslau: Schottlaender, 1894). *Werde* was reprinted in 1977 (Frankfurt: Arndtstraße). Another reprint edited by Berta Rahm was published in 1988 (Neunkirch: Ala).

3. "Die alte Frau," *Die Zukunft*, no. 12 (1903): 22–30. Edited by Maximilian Harden. Berlin. Reprinted in *Zur Psychologie der Frau*, edited and introduction by Gisela Brinker-Gabler, 210–20 (Frankfurt am Main: Fischer Taschenbuch Verlag, 1978).

1. Sappho was the poet-priestess of Lesbos, the "isle of women." The *Fliegende Blätter* was a humorous journal of caricatures, poems, and stories published in Munich from 1844–1944.

2. Psyche is Greek for "female soul." Classical mythology wedded Psyche to the love-god Eros. Their marriage was a union of the soul with the body.

3. Mignon is a young girl (12–13 years old) who is first encountered in Goethe's *Wilhelm Meisters Lehrjahre*. She accompanies Wilhelm after he buys her freedom, later becoming very ill from homesickness for her native country, Italy.

4. *Mämmchen*: the diminutive form "chen" can be understood as belittling or pejorative; however, it also denotes a form of endearment.

5. Arnold Böcklin (1827–1901) was born in Basel, Switzerland; he was trained in Düsseldorf. He is referred to as a "German Roman" because of the many years he spent in Italy.

6. Charlotte Corday (1768–1793) was a moderate Girondin in the French Revolution; she murdered the more radical Jean Paul Marat. Immediately apprehended, she was sentenced to death and executed on July 17, 1793.

7. Raphael (1483–1520) was master painter and architect of the Italian High Renaissance.

8. Tiberius (born 42 B.C., died A.D. 37) was Roman emperor from A.D. 14–37. He went to live on Capri in A.D. 26 and ruled in absentia.

9. The greatest living philosopher refers to Friedrich Nietzsche and his theory of the "Übermensch."

10. Jean Paul (1763–1825) was a German author. Real name: Jean Paul Friedrich Richter.

"The Old Woman"

1. Moltke (1800–1891) was a Prussian General Field Marshall.

1. For biographical information on Dohm, see biographies by Adele Schreiber, *Hedwig Dohm als Vorkämpferin und Vordenkerin neuer Frauenideale* (Berlin: Märkische Verlagsanstaalt, 1914); Julia Meißner, *Mehr Stolz Ihr Frauen! Hedwig Dohm—eine Biographie* (Düsseldorf: Schwann, 1987); and Heike Brandt, *"Die Menschenrechte haben kein Geschlecht." Lebensgeschichte der Hedwig Dohm* (Weinheim: Belz and Gelberg, 1989).

2. Meißner, *Mehr Stolz*, 17.

3. See her essay, reprinted in: *Erinnerungen an Hedwig Dohm*, edited by Berta Rahm (Zürich: Ala, 1980), 45–78.

4. "Zehn von ihren achtzehn Kindern nährte die Mutter selbst. Ich war das erste ihrer Ammenkinder. Darum mochte sie mich nicht. Ich weiss es von ihr selbst" [Mother breast-fed ten of her eighteen children herself. I was the first of her wet-nurse children. That's why she didn't like me. I know this from her directly.] ("Kindheitserinnerungen," 65).

5. She discusses this in other works as well. For example, also see: *Was die Pastoren denken* [What the Pastors think] (Berlin: Reinhold Schlingmann, 1872). Reprinted and introduction by Berta Rahm (Zürich: Ala, 1977), 44–45.

6. See Meißner, *Mehr Stolz*, 40.

7. Elke Frederiksen writes: "Als Mutter von fünf Kindern spielte sie zunächst eine recht passive Rolle an diesen geselligen Abenden und litt besonders an ihrer mangelnden Ausbildung. Doch durch eifriges Zuhören und Lesen bildete sie sich selbst und fing schließlich sogar zu schreiben an" [As mother of five children, she played a rather passive role in this social evenings in the beginning and especially suffered because of her lack of education. However, through zealous listening and reading, she educated herself and finally even began to write]. *Die Frauenfrage in Deutschland 1865–1915: Texte und Dokumente* (Stuttgart: Reclam, 1981), 466.

8. "Das Stillschweigen, das Hedwig Dohm hartnäckig über ihre Ehe und Ernst Dohm bewahrte, legt die Vermutung nahe, daß das Zusammenleben, wenigstens für Hedwigs Empfinden, nicht ohne tiefere

Probleme war" [The silence about her marriage and Ernst Dohm that Hedwig Dohm stubbornly adhered to leads to the conjecture that their life together, at least for Hedwig's feelings, was not without deeper problems] (32).

9. Dohm was called "Mimchen" by her daughters and their families.

10. "Erinnerungen an Hedwig Dohm." In: *Erinnerungen*, pp. 11–37. This quote, p. 16.

11. Reprinted in *Erinnerungen*, 197–200.

12. For the differing perspectives among various wings of the women's movement on the topic of suffrage, education, women and work, and women's role in the family see, for example, Frederiksen, *Die Frauenfrage*, or Richard J. Evans, *The Feminist Movement in Germany 1894–1933* (London: SAGE, 1976).

13. Dohm, *Der Frauen Natur und Recht. Zur Frauenfrage zwei Abhandlungen über Eigenschaften und Stimmrecht der Frauen* [Woman's Nature and Privilege. About the Women's Question Two Treatises on Women's Attributes and Right to Vote] (Berlin: Wedekind and Schwieger, 1876). Reprinted in Berta Rahm (Neunkirch: Ala, 1986), 185. Dohm ended this book on women's rights and the right to vote with the quoted (revolutionary) statement.

14. Gaby Pailer, *Schreibe, die du bist. Die Gestaltung weiblicher "Autorschaft" im erzählerischen Werk Hedwig Dohms* (Pfaffenweiler: Centaurus, 1994), 14–15.

15. See pages 14–15, especially footnotes 25–28.

16. For examples of studies on madness and hysteria in women at the turn of the century, see: Elaine Showalter, *The Female Malady: Women, Madness, and English Culture, 1830–1980* (NY: Penquin, 1985); Sandra M. Gilbert and Susan Gubar, *Madwomen in the Attic: The Woman Writer and the Nineteenth-Century Literary Imagination* (New Haven: Yale University Press, 1979); Marianne Schuller, "'Weibliche Neurose' und Identität. Zur Diskussion der Hysterie um die Jahrhundertwende," in *Die Wiederkehr des Körpers*, eds. Dietmar Kamper and Christoph Wulf, 180–92 (Frankfurt am Main: Suhrkamp, 1982); or specifically about Dohm: Lilo Weber, *"Fliegen und Zittern: Hysterie in Texten von Theodor*

Fontane, Hedwig Dohm, Gabriele Reuter und Minna Kautsky (Bielefeld: Aisthyesis, 1996), 143–95. Freud, of course, also influenced this line of thought with his study of women in his psychoanalytic work. The young Viennese lecturer Otto Weininger also provides an interesting footnote to this discussion with his misogynist views in *Sex and Character (Geschlecht und Charakter)*, (1903).

17. *Die Mütter. Beitrag zur Erziehungsfrage* [Mothers. Contribution to the Question of Education] (Berlin: S. Fischer, 1903).

18. For more details on Dohm's ideas about the traditional view of mothers-in-law and the role that they will play in the future, see her chapter, "Die Schwiegermutter der Zukunft" [The Mother-in-Law of the Future], in *Die Mütter*, 189–200.

19. The painting by Antoine Wiertz (Musées des Royaux des Beaus-Arts / Musée Wiertz, Brussels) provides the cover for Gaby Pailer's book *Schreibe, die du bist*.

20. For example, Arthur Schnitzler and James Joyce.

21. For eighteenth- and nineteenth-century women writers and their "nontraditional" genres, see for example: *Literatur von Frauen*, edited by Gisela Brinker-Gabler (Munich: Beck, 1988). Vol. I: *Vom Mittelalter bis zum Ende des 18. Jahrhunderts* and Vol. II: *19. und 20. Jahrhundert*. See also: *Frauen Literatur Geschichte. Schreibende Frauen vom Mittelalter bis zur Gegenwart*, edited by Hiltrud Gnüg and Renate Möhrmann (Stuttgart: Suhrkamp, 1989).

22. Elisabeth Plessen, "Hedwig Dohm (1833 [sic]–1919): Kein Stimmrecht—kein Recht zu lieben!" in: *Frauen Porträts aus zwei Jahrhunderten*, edited by Hans Jürgen Schultz (Stuttgart: Kreuz, 1981), 128–31, here: 137.

23. See her articles on Dohm: "The Ambiguous World of Hedwig Dohm," *Amsterdamer Beiträge zur neueren Germanistik* (Amsterdam, Rodopi, 1980), 255–76; and "Die Zaehmung der alten Frau bei Hedwig Dohm," *Die widerspenstige Zähmung. Studien zur bezwungenen Weiblichkeit in der Literatur vom Mittelalter bis zur Gegenwart*, eds. Sylvia Wallinger and Monika Jonas (Innsbruck: Universität, 1986), 217–27.

24. Joeres writes: "[...] sowohl die Charaktere als auch die Erzählerin [wirken] oft verunsichert und unklar" [...the characters as

well as the narrator often seem insecure and unclear] ("Die Zähmung der alten Frau bei Hedwig Dohm," 217).

25. For summaries of this topic, see, for example, the chapter "Mädchenerziehung und Frauenbildung," in Frederiksen, *Die Frauenfrage*; or see: Laura Tate, "The Culture of Literary *Bildung* in the Bourgeois Women's Movement in Imperial Germany," *German Studies Review* 24.2 (May 2001): 267–81.

26. See chapter three: "Anregungen zur Erziehungsfrage" [Ideas for the Education Question], 77ff.

27. Ute Speck, *Ein Mögliches Ich. Selbstreflexion in der Schreiberfahrung. Zur Autobiographik der Politikerinnen Lily Braun, Hedwig Dohm und Rosa Luxemburg* (Frankfurt am Main: Peter Lang, 1997), 193.

Bibliography

Works by Hedwig Dohm

Die Spanische National-Literatur in ihrer geschichtlichen Entwickelung: Nebst den Lebens- und Charakterbildern ihrer classischen Schriftsteller und Proben aus den Werken derselben in deutscher Übertragung. 2 Vols. Berlin: Gustav Hempel, 1867.

Was die Pastoren von den Frauen denken. Berlin and Leipzig: Schlingmann, 1872. Reprint as *Was die Pastoren denken.* Zürich: Ala, 1977.

Der Jesuitismus im Hausstande. Ein Beitrag zur Frauenfrage. Berlin: Wedekind and Schwieger, 1873. Reprint in *Der Frauen Natur und Recht.* 2d ed., 1893.

Die wissenschaftliche Emancipation der Frau. Berlin: Wedekind and Schwieger, 1874, 1877. Reprint in *Der Frauen Natur und Recht*, 2d ed., 1893. Reprint as *Emanzipation*, 2d ed. Zürich: Ala, 1982.

Der Frauen Natur und Recht. Zur Frauenfrage. Zwei Abhandlungen über Eigenschaften und Stimmrecht der Frauen. Berlin: Wedekind and Schwieger, 1876. Expanded 2d edition includes *Der Jesuitismus im Hausstande* and *Die wissenschaftliche Emancipation der Frau.* Berlin: Stahn, 1893. Reprint as *Der Frauen Natur und Recht.* Neunkirch: Ala, 1986.

Der Seelenretter. Lustspiel. Berlin: Eduard Krause, 1875. Wien: Verlag der Wallishausser'schen Buchhandlung, 1876.

Vom Stamm der Asra. Lustspiel. Berlin: Lassar's Buchhandlung, 1876. Berlin: Eduard Bloch, 1876.

Ein Schuß in's Schwarze. Lustspiel. Erfurt: Friedrich Bartholomäus, 1878.

Die Ritter vom goldenen Kalb. Lustspiel. Berlin: R. Gensch, 1878. Berlin: Eduard Bloch, 1879.

Lust und Leid im Liede: Neuere deutsche Lyrik. Edited by Hedwig Dohm and F. Brunold. Leipzig and Berlin: Albrecht, 1879. 7th ed. Berlin: Steinitz, 1887.

Frau Tannhäuser. Novellen. Breslau: Schottlaender, 1890.

Plein Air. Roman. Berlin: Lehmann, 1891.

Wie Frauen werden. Werde, die Du bist. Novellen. Breslau: Schottlaender, 1894. Reprinted as *Werde, die du bist.* Frankfurt am Main: Verlag Arndtstraße, 1977.

Sibilla Dalmar. Roman aus dem Ende unseres Jahrhunderts. Berlin: S. Fischer, 1896, 1897.

Schicksale einer Seele. Roman. Berlin: S. Fischer, 1899. Reprint, edited by Ruth-Ellen Boetcher Joeres. Munich: Frauenoffensive, 1988.

Die Antifeministen: Ein Buch der Verteidigung. Berlin: Dümmler, 1902, 1907. Reprint, Frankfurt: Verlag Arndtstraße, 1976.

Christa Ruland. Roman. Berlin: S. Fischer, 1902.

Die Mütter: Beitrag zur Erziehungsfrage. Berlin: S. Fischer, 1903.

"Die alte Frau." *Die Zukunft,* no. 12 (1903): 22–30. Edited by Maximilian Harden. Berlin. Reprinted in *Zur Psychologie der Frau,* edited and introduction by Gisela Brinker-Gabler, 210–20. Frankfurt am Main: Fischer Taschenbuch Verlag, 1978.

Schwanenlieder. Berlin: S. Fischer, 1906.

Erziehung zum Stimmrecht der Frau. Schriften des Preußischen Landesvereins für Frauenstimmrecht 6. Berlin: Selbstverlag, 1909, 1910, 1914.

Sommerlieben. Freiluftnovellen. Berlin: Vita, 1909, 1910. Reprint, Frankfurt am Main: Ulrike Helmer, 1990.

Ehe? Zur Reform der sexuellen Moral. Eds. Hedwig Dohm, Anita Augspurg, Helene Stöcker, et al. Berlin: Internationale Verlagsanstalt, 1911.

"Aphorismen." *Ehe? Zur Reform der sexuellen Moral,* 15–17.

"Zur sexuellen Moral der Frau." *Ehe? Zur Reform der sexuellen Moral,* 7–14.

"Kindheitserinnerungen einer alten Berlinerin." *Als unsere großen Dichterinnen noch kleine Mädchen waren: Selbsterzählte Jugenderinnerungen.* Eds. Ida Boy-Ed, Hedwig Dohm, Enrica Handel-Manzetti, et al, 17–57. Leipzig and Berlin: Franz Moeser Nachfolger, 1912. Reprint in *Erinnerungen,* edited by Berta Rahm, 45–78. Zürich: Ala, 1980.

"Mutter und Großmutter." In *Mutterschaft: Ein Sammelwerk für die Probleme des Weibes als Mutter.* Edited by Adele Schreiber, 649–61. Munich: Albert Langen, 1912.

"Der Mißbrauch des Todes. Senile Impressionen." In *Das Aktionsbuch.* Edited by Franz Pfemfert, 95–112. Berlin-Wilmersdorf: Verlag Die Aktion, 1917. *Der Missbrauch des Todes. Senile Impressionen.* Vol. 2 of *Der rote Hahn.* Edited by Franz Pfemfert. Berlin-Wilmersdorf: Verlag Die Aktion, 1918. Reprint, Düsseldorf: Zwiebelzwerg, 1986.

Periodical Publications

Hedwig Dohm contributed journalistic, essayistic, and fictional works to many journals, including: *Nord und Süd, Westermanns Illustrirte Deutsche Monatshefte, Die Zukunft, Die Zeit. Wiener Wochenschrift für Politik, Volkswirtschaft, Wissenschaft und Kunst, Die Woche, Bühne und Welt, Die Gesellschaft. Halbmonatsschrift für Literatur, Kunst und Sozialpolitik, Die Frauenbewegung, Die Frau, Bühne und Welt, Sozialistische Montashefte, Die Aktion, Litterarische Echo. Halbmonatsschrift für Literaturfreunde, Die Staatsbürgerin. Monatsschrift des Deutschen Verbandes für Frauenstimmrecht.*

Secondary Literature

Brandt, Heike. *"Die Menschenrechte haben kein Geschlecht": Die Lebensgeschichte der Hedwig Dohm."* Weinheim: Beltz and Gelberg, 1989.

Brinker-Gabler, Gisela, ed. "Die Frau ohne Eigenschaften." Hedwig Dohms Roman. *Christa Ruland. Feministische Studien* 3.1 (1984): 117–27.

———. *Deutsche Literatur von Frauen.* 2 Vols. Munich: C. H. Beck, 1988.

———. "Perspektiven des Übergangs. Weibliches Bewußtsein und frühe Moderne." In Vol. 2 of *Deutsche Literatur von Frauen.* Edited by Gisela Brinker-Gabler, 69–205. Munich: C. H. Beck, 1988.

Burkhard, Marianne, ed. *Gestaltet und Gestaltend: Frauen in der deutschen Literatur.* Amsterdamer Beiträge zur neueren Germanistik 10. Amsterdam: Rodopi, 1980.

Duelli-Klein, Renate. "Hedwig Dohm: Passionate Theorist (1833 [*sic*]–1919)." In *Feminist Theorists: Three Centuries of Women's Intellectual Traditions*. Edited by Dale Spender, 165–83. London: The Women's Press, 1983.

Evans, Richard J. *The Feminist Movement in Germany 1894–1933*. London: SAGE, 1976.

Frederiksen, Elke, ed. *Die Frauenfrage in Deutschland 1865–1915: Texte und Dokumente*. Stuttgart: Reclam, 1981.

——— and Elizabeth G. Ametsbichler, eds. *Women Writers in German-Speaking Countries. A Bio-Bibliographical Critical Sourcebook*. Westport, CT: Greenwood, 1998.

Giesing, Michaela. "Theater als verweigerter Raum. Dramatikerinnen der Jahrhundertwende in deutschsprachigen Ländern." In *Schreibende Frauen. Frauen Literatur Geschichte vom Mittelalter bis zur Gegenwart*. Edited by Hiltrud Gnüg and Renate Möhrmann, 240–59. Stuttgart: Suhrkamp, 1989.

Gilbert, Sandra M., and Susan Gubar. *Madwomen in the Attic: The Woman Writer and the Nineteenth-Century Literary Imagination*. New Haven, CT: Yale University Press, 1979.

Gnüg, Hiltrud and Renate Möhrmann, eds. *Frauen Literatur Geschichte: Schreibende Frauen vom Mittelalter bis zur Gegenwart*. Stuttgart: Suhrkamp, 1989.

Joeres, Ruth. "The Ambiguous World of Hedwig Dohm." In *Gestaltet und Gestaltend. Frauen in der deutschen Literatur*. Edited by Marianne Burkhard. Amsterdamer Beiträge zur neueren Germanistik 10, 255–76. Amsterdam: Rodopi, 1980.

———. "Die Nebensächlichen: Selbstbehauptung durch Protest in den Schriften deutscher Schriftstellerinnen im 19. Jahrhundert." In *Frauensprache—Frauenliteratur? Für und Wider einer Psychoanalyse literarischer Werke*. Edited by Inge Stephan and Carl Pietzcker. Vol. 6 of *Kontroversen, alte und neue*. Akten des VII. Internationalen Germanisten-Kongresses Göttingen 1985, 68–72. Tübingen: Niemeyer, 1986.

———. "Die Zähmung der alten Frau: Hedwig Dohms *Werde, die du bist*." In *Die Widerspenstigen Zähmung. Studien zur bezwungenen Weiblichkeit in der Literatur vom Mittelalter bis zur Gegenwart*. Edited by Silvia Wallinger and Monika Jonas, 217–28. Innsbruck: Universität, 1986.

———. "Die 'Fremdlinge der Menschheit': 'Schicksale einer Seele' als Frauenporträt." Afterword to *Schicksale einer Seele*. Edited by

Ruth-Ellen Boetcher Joeres, 129–35. Munich: Frauenoffensive, 1988.

———. "Hedwig Dohm." In *Women Writers in German-Speaking Countries. A Bio-Bibliographical Critical Sourcebook*. Edited by Elke P. Frederiksen and Elizabeth G. Ametsbichler, 86–95. Westport, CT: Greenwood, 1998.

———. *Respectability and Deviance: Nineteenth-Century German Women Writers and the Ambiguity of Representation*. Chicago: University of Chicago Press, 1998.

Kaloyanova-Slavova, Ludmila. *Übergangsgeschöpfe: Gabriele Reuter, Hedwig Dohm, Helene Böhlau und Franziska von Reventlow*. New York: Peter Lang, 1998.

Kamper, Dieter and Christoph Wulf, eds. *Die Wiederkehr des Körpers*. Frankfurt am Main: Suhrkamp, 1982.

Meißner, Julia. *Mehr Stolz, Ihr Frauen! Hedwig Dohm—eine Biographie*. Düsseldorf: Schwann, 1987.

Müller, Nikola. *Hedwig Dohm (1831–1919): Eine kommentierte Bibliografie*. Berlin: trafo verlag dr. wolfgang weist, 2000.

Pailer, Gaby. *Schreibe, die du bist. Die Gestaltung weiblicher "Autorschaft" im erzählerischen Werk Hedwig Dohms*. Pfaffenweiler: Centaurus, 1994.

——— and Vera Stober. "Hedwig Dohm 'weibliches Schreiben' als respektloses Plagiat männlicher Schriftkultur." In *Frauen—Literatur—Revolution*. Edited by Helga Grubitzsch, Maria Kublitz, Dorothea Mey, and Ingeborg Singendonk-Heublein, 173–84. Pfaffenweiler: Centaurus, 1992.

Plessen, Elisabeth. "Hedwig Dohm (1833 [sic]–1919)." In *Frauen Porträts aus zwei Jahrhunderten*. Edited by Hans-Jürgen Schulz, 128–41. Stuttgart: Kreuz, 1982.

Rahm, Berta, ed. *Erinnerungen*. Includes: Hedda Korsch "Erinnerungen an Hedwig Dohm" and Hedwig Dohm "Jugenderinnerungen einer alten Berlinerin" as well as other texts by and about Hedwig Dohm. Zürich: Ala, 1980.

Reed, Philippa. "Vom 'Angel in the House' zur 'neuen Frau.'" In *Frauensprache—Frauenliteratur? Für und Wider einer Psychoanalyse literarischer Werke*. Edited by Inge Stephan and Carl Pietzcker. Vol. 6 of *Kontroversen, alte und neue*. Akten des VII. Internationalen Germanisten-Kongresses Göttingen 1985, 78–86. Tübingen: Max Niemeyer, 1986.

Schreiber, Adele. *Hedwig Dohm als Vorkämpferin und Vordenkerin neuer Frauenideale*. Berlin: Märkische Verlagsanstalt, 1914.

Schuller, Marianne. "'Weibliche Neurose' und Identität. Zur Diskussion der Hysterie um die Jahrhundertwende." In *Die Wiederkehr des Körpers*. Edited by Dietmar Kamper and Christoph Wulf, 180–192. Frankfurt am Main: Suhrkamp, 1982.

Schulz, Hans-Jürgen, ed. *Frauen Porträts aus zwei Jahrhunderten*. Stuttgart: Kreuz, 1982.

Showalter, Elaine. *The Female Malady. Women, Madness, and English Culture, 1830–1980*. NY: Penquin, 1985.

Specht, Ute. *Ein Mögliches Ich. Selbstreflexion in der Schreiberfahrung. Zur Autobiographik der Politikerinnen Lily Braun, Hedwig Dohm und Rosa Luxemburg*. Frankfurt am Main: Peter Lang, 1997.

Stephan, Inge and Carl Pietzcker, eds. *Frauensprache—Frauenliteratur? Für und Wider einer Psychoanalyse literarischer Werke*. Vol. 6 of *Kontroversen, alte und neue*. Akten des VII. Internationalen Germanisten-Kongresses Göttingen 1985. Tübingen: Max Niemeyer, 1986.

Tate, Laura. "The Culture of Literary *Bildung* in the Bourgeois Women's Movement in Imperial Germany." In *German Studies Review* 24.2 (May 2001): 267–81.

Wallinger, Silvia and Monika Jonas, eds. *Die Widerspenstigen Zähmung: Studien zur bezwungenen Weiblichkeit in der Literatur vom Mittelalter bis zur Gegenwart*. Innsbruck: Universität, 1986.

Weber, Lilo. *"Fliegen und Zittern." Hysterie in Texten von Theodor Fontane, Hedwig Dohm, Gabriele Reuter und Minna Kautsky*, 143–95. Bielefeld: Aisthesis, 1966.

Weedon, Chris. "The Struggle for Women's Emancipation in the Work of Hedwig Dohm." In *German Life and Letters*, no. 37 (1994): 182–92.

Zepler, Wally, "Hedwig Dohm." In *Sozialistische Monatshefte*, no. 3.19 (1913): 1292–1301.

Index

Mämmchen, 18, 20, 21, 24
Mann, Thomas, ix
Marie Antoinette, 2, 26
Marlitt, 11, 16
marriage, 11, 12, 13, 14, 36, 83, 88
matromania, 58
mechanical: daily life, 60; housework, 56; movement, 7; reading, 16; speech, 21
medicine, women in, 20, 21, 98
Medussa, 6
megalomania, 38
Meißner, Julia, 83
melancholy, 1, 49, 62
memoir, 81
memory, 17, 44, 78; of adolescence, 44, 82; of childhood, 82; painful, 82; weakness of, 72
Menschenrechte haben kein Geschlecht, Die, 85
mental: confusion, 25; disturbance, 1; hospital, 1, 86; longevity, 77, 100; strength, 61, 77, 93; vigor, 70
metaphor, 91
Mignon, 18; old Mignon, 30, 97
Mimchen, 83
mind, 77, 78, 82; clarity of, 87; disturbed, 3, 7, 87; German patriotic, 75; state of, 78, 92
mirror, 16, 20, 22, 26, 44
misery, 49, 54, 64
Moltke, 76
moon, 10, 56
moonlight, 78
moral, 24, 25, 72; elite, 36
mortal, 78
Moses, 43, 97
mother, 19, 21, 69, 71, 75; of man, 70
mother-in-law, 19, 20, 21, 22, 71; anecdotes, 22
mother of God, 54
motif, 90, 91
mourning, 15

Mütter, Die, 90, 98
myrtle, 62, 63; wreath, 3, 4, 6, 11, 62, 63, 65, 94; thorny myrtle wreath, 66

national differences, 75
natural law, 34; household of, 71; limits, of, 79; wild, 78
nature, 9, 39, 41, 42, 47, 52, 58; chained-up, 32, 90
Neptune, 47, 49, 53
Nereids, 52
nerves, 13, 56, 62, 79, 100; brain's, 33; cranial, 78; shattered, 18, 89; strained, 43
nervous: shaking, 31; state, 90; system (sensitive), 7
nervousness, 13, 15, 18, 19, 24, 31
New Testament, 97
Nietzsche, 1, 86, 99
nineteenth century, 98; males, 91; women, 95, 99
nonfiction, x, 97, 98, 99
norms, social, 89, 98, 99
North Sea, 38, 62, 91
novel(s), autobiographical, 83
novella, xi, 81, 83, 85, 86, 87, 89, 91, 92, 98, 99
nursery, 71, 72

oblivion, 68
old, age, 31, 39, 70, 73, 74; lady, 4, 23, 73, 86; man, 8, 30, 69, 73, 75, 76, 93, 97; men, 87; mother, 74; ones, 74, 77; people, 70; person, 72; the 73; witch, 70
Old Testament, 97
"Old Woman," xi, 67–79, 70, 86, 87, 89, 90, 91, 97, 98, 100
old woman, 1, 2, 4–8, 16, 18, 30, 31, 34, 39, 61, 63–65, 67–71, 73–79, 89, 90, 92–95, 97, 100; as burden, 69, 74; as monster, 74; American,

75; English, 75; German, 75; Norwegian, 75
old women, 87, 94
On Death's Bed (1919, After the World War of 1914–1918), 84
opportunity, for women, 10, 75, 88, 95
order, social, 74
orthography, 10, 82, 96

pacifist, 85
Pailer, Gaby, 86, 91, 96
pain, 49, 60
pamphlet, 84
paranoia, 18, 21, 90
pariah, of humankind, 67
Parnassus, 47
passing of time, 45
passionflower, 4, 7, 55, 56, 59, 63, 65
patience, 72
patriarchy: patriarchal arguments, x; patriarchal society, 98; patriarchal thinking, 99
physical, 93, 94; activity, 82; awkwardness, 72; deeds, 87; end, 95; limitations, 82; strength, 72
piety, 72
Pindar, 86, 99
pioneer, x
Pitti Palace, 45
planet(s), 42, 49
Plessen, Elisabeth, 96
poem, 50
poet, 50
poetess, 1, 6
poetic splendor, 54
poetry, 52, 56, 57
polemic(s), 90, 96, 97
power, 34, 37, 58, 63, 71; of spring, 57
prejudice, 70, 76, 90
priestly, 76
Pringsheim, Katia, ix
prison, 69; life-long, 35
Privy Councilor, 2, 87

prophetic, 8
prose, 86
Psyche, 6, 64; Grandmother Psyche, 64, 94

quest, 87, 91, 92, 97, 98, 99

radical, x
Raphael, 42
reading, 11, 13, 16, 24–25, 33, 88, 90, 91
reason, 32, 36–37, 45, 85, 86, 98
rebellion, 98
relationships: between older man and younger woman, 87, 93; between older woman and younger man, 87, 93; erotic, 87; grandmother/grandchildren: Agnes/grandchildren, 20, 23, 71, 72, 90; Dohm/grandchildren, 83, 84, 90; familial, 85; husband/wife: 11; Agnes/Eduard, 12, 17, 22, 32; Magdalene/Eugen, 22, 36; Hedwig/Ernst, 83; marital, 85; mother/child, 2, 24, 32, 33, 89, 90; mother/daughter: 71, 72, 89, 90; Agnes/mother, 10, 11; Agnes/daughter(s), 3, 13, 17, 18, 19, 22, 89; Hedwig Dohm/mother, 81–82; mother-in-law/son-in-law: 71; Agnes/sons-in-law, 18, 19, 20, 21, 22, 23, 24, 90, 98; parent/children, 11, 84
religious law, 97
repression, 86, 87, 89
resignation, 62, 95
resistance, 34, 46, 90, 95, 98
rest, 15, 88
restlessness, 3, 8, 15, 17, 21, 38, 88
restriction(s), 95
revenge, 35
reverence, 72
Revolution of 1848, 84
riddle of the universe (*Weltseele*), 37, 52

ridicule, 76, 77, 87, 90, 94, 98
rights: of the aging, 85; of existence, 79; of mother, 67, 71; of old woman, 7, 23; of wife, 67; of woman, ix, 67; of young girl, 67, 93
role model, xi
rules, of aesthetics, 76

sacrifice, 74
sacrificial, 58; flame, 4; lamb, 94
sad, 14, 23, 45
sadness, 43, 49, 66
salon, 73, 82
sanitarium, 7, 23, 94, 95
sanity, 24, 90
San Michele, 44, 49, 51
San Miniato, 44, 46
sapere aude, 85
Sappho, 6, 64, 94
sarcasm, 72
Savior, 8, 94
Schiller, 10
Schleh, 81
Schleh, Hedwig, 82
Schlesinger, Gustav Adolph Gott-hold, 81
Schicksale einer Seele, 81, 84
schooling, 10
Schreibe, die du bist, 86, 96
Schreiber, Adele, x
Scientific Emancipation of the Woman, 83
sea, 4, 5–6, 35, 38–43, 46, 49, 50, 52–56, 58, 61–63, 94; foam, 40, 62
search, 1, 3, 17, 18, 27, 54, 70, 85, 87, 89, 92, 95, 96, 98, 99, 100
seer, 1, 38
self: awareness, 95; confident, 95; determination, 95; detriment of, 99; exploration, 95; image, 92; inner, 56; quest for, 87, 99, 100; revelation, 95; sense of, 89, 91; unfinished, 39; worth, 86

sewing, 11, 54; machine, 13, 17, 88
sexual: appeal, 68, 70; being, 73; worth, 67
shadow(s), 9, 37, 65, 66, 67, 71, 75
shadow-like, 4
shame, 10, 60, 61, 68, 78, 93
shroud, 68
Sibilla Dalmar, 81, 84
Sicily, 49
sick, 14, 46, 54, 56
sickbed, 14
sickness, 23, 49
Siegfried, 7, 26
signifier, 97
silence, 68
Silesian dialect, 73
Sinai, 43, 97
Sirens, the, 4, 62, 63
sky, 10, 29, 33, 40, 41, 47, 48, 52, 61, 65; gray, 27; star-filled (heavens), 34
snake(s), 59, 63
social: comedies, 83; confines, 92; connections, 74; constraints, 89; constrictions, 90; construction, 99; culture, 73; customs, 86, 97; habits, 86; ideals, 97; justice, 84; law, 97; life, 79,100; norms, 89, 98; order, 74; prejudice, 90; reality, 93
society, x, 69, 70, 73, 77, 85, 86, 88, 90, 91, 92, 93; patriarchal, 98
son/daughter treatment, 9, 10, 11, 82
soul, 2, 4, 25, 38, 41, 51, 53, 69, 71, 75, 78, 82, 92; beauty, 61, 94; con-nection, 94; flaming, 43; housewife, 35; kisses (from soul to soul), 60, 93; murder of, 42, 92; transmigra-tion of, 25; wedding (of two souls), 58; world (*Weltseele*), 35, 51, 52, 60
sparks, 33, 52
Speck, Ute, 99
spirits, 41, 78
spiritual life, 35
stars, 25, 37, 49, 50, 51; silent, 69

storm, 41, 42, 46, 52
story, 61, 90; frame, 86, 89, 93, 94;
    inner, 87, 89; personal (Agnes
    Schmidt's), 87
suffer, 31
suicidal thoughts, 43
suicide, 42
sun, 12, 26, 30, 35, 37, 39, 42, 44, 49,
    55, 56, 57, 59, 62; pale, 41; setting,
    65, 70
superfluous(ness), 68, 73, 74, 79, 89
swan song, 43, 65
Switzerland, 14
sympathy, 72

tears, 42; of fire, 58; of passion, 64; of
    Tiberius, 64
Ten Commandments, 97
theater, 83, 90
theoretical writings/works, 82, 84, 90,
    96, 97, 98
thinking, x, 32, 50, 88, 92; forward,
    85; patriarchal, 99
thought, x, 1, 7, 13, 14, 17, 21, 25, 30,
    31, 33, 34, 36–38, 41, 44, 46, 50,
    55, 60, 64, 71, 88, 90, 93, 95, 98;
    suicidal, 43
Tiber, ghost of, 63
Tiberius, 55, 58; ghost of, 63; ruins of,
    54, 61; sin of, 59; tears of, 64
Tolstoy, 56
tombs, 46
tradition, x, 91; literary, 99; literary
    (male, German), 91
transitoriness, 48
travel, 2, 14, 23, 35, 36, 37, 75, 77, 88,
    90, 91
treatise(s), 83
trilogy, 83
truth, inner, 93
Turgenev, 69
turning point, 84
Tyrol, 14

unconsciousness, 5
unhappiness, 41
universe, 40, 49, 51
upper classes, 75

vanity, 25
Varnhagen, Karl August, 82
veil, 3, 11, 59; flaming, 47
Vesuvius, 58
victim, 41
Virgin Mary, 54
vision(s), 9, 34, 41, 43, 60, 92, 95;
    democratic, 85
Volksfest, 29–30, 90

wander, 32, 38, 39, 47, 54
wandering, 37; wanderlust, 35; Völker-
    wanderung, 25
*Was die Pastoren von den Frauen
    denken*, 83
weakness, 72
wealth, 70
wed, 65
wedding, 12
Werde, die du bist, xi, 81, 82, 83–84, 85
What the Pastors think About
    Women, 83
white dress, 76
white (gray) hair, 26, 43, 56, 57,
    77–78, 87
widow(s), 8, 9, 19, 20, 42, 85, 89, 91
widow-burning, 6, 91
wife, of man, 70
will, 71
Wilmersdorf, 28
wings, 29, 38, 55, 92
*wissenschaftliche Emancipation der Frau,
    Die*, 83
wit, x, 96, 97
witch, 70; old, 70
witches' Sabbath, 59
woman, 79; as ballast, 68; creative, 72;
    enlightened, 95; matronly, 71

womanhood, 91
womb, 39, 51; of the mountains, 29, 47, 51
women, nineteenth-century, ix, 95, 99
women's: imprisonment, 91; issues, ix, x, 85; movement, x, 79, 84, 98; plight, 85; position: in the home, 85; in society, 85; rights: 67; activists, 84; role: 25, 43, 89; as bearer of children, 67, 74; as daughter, 88; as caretaker, 67, 99; as grandmother, 88; as housewife, 92; as lover, 67; as mother, 88; as mother-in-law, 88; as raiser of children, 74; as wife, 88; suffrage, 84; worth, 68, 74
Women's Nature and Privilege, 85
World War I, 85

wreath(s), 3, 46, 59; bridal, 3, 94; wilted, 4
Write Who You Are, 86
writer(s), ix, 42, 83, 84, 91, 98
writing, x, 7, 8, 9, 18, 35, 37, 48, 65, 78, 85, 90, 95, 96, 97
writings, ix

yearning, 34, 36, 43, 60, 92
young, 44, 57; gentleman, 73; girl(s), 29, 39, 61; maiden, 6; man, 74, 77; woman, 1, 30, 31, 69, 93; women, 87; people, 29
youth, 12, 30, 37, 61, 75, 76, 79, 92, 93, 94, 100; aesthetic joy of, 61, 68; dead, 58

Zarathustra, 1
Zola, 69
zoo, 27